Clint lowered his head and plowed on to the huge cage

with the night crew. It was just a cage, but with a welded bar all around to hang onto. Clint noticed most of the crew were crowded into the center of the cage.

Bob Fortney pushed in last. "Better hang on tight, Octojock!"

Clint just smiled as if he didn't understand. But when the earth dropped out from under his feet and he plunged into absolute darkness he had to choke back a scream, and he clamped on with both hands.

Down, down, down they fell. For Clint, it was like a journey into hell. He couldn't help thinking he'd made a terrible mistake....

Don't miss any of the lusty, hard-riding action in
the Charter Western series, THE GUNSMITH

1. MACKLIN'S WOMEN
2. THE CHINESE GUNMAN
3. THE WOMAN HUNT
4. THE GUNS OF ABILENE
5. THREE GUNS FOR GLORY
6. LEADTOWN
7. THE LONGHORN WAR
8. QUANAH'S REVENGE
9. HEAVYWEIGHT GUN
10. NEW ORLEANS FIRE
11. ONE-HANDED GUN
12. THE CANADIAN PAYROLL
13. DRAW TO AN INSIDE DEATH
14. DEAD MAN'S HAND
15. BANDIT GOLD
16. BUCKSKINS AND SIX-GUNS
17. SILVER WAR
18. HIGH NOON AT LANCASTER
19. BANDIDO BLOOD
20. THE DODGE CITY GANG
21. SASQUATCH HUNT
22. BULLETS AND BALLOTS
23. THE RIVERBOAT GANG
24. KILLER GRIZZLY
25. NORTH OF THE BORDER
26. EAGLE'S GAP
27. CHINATOWN HELL
28. THE PANHANDLE SEARCH
29. WILDCAT ROUNDUP
30. THE PONDEROSA WAR
31. TROUBLE RIDES A FAST HORSE
32. DYNAMITE JUSTICE
33. THE POSSE
34. NIGHT OF THE GILA
35. THE BOUNTY WOMEN
36. BLACK PEARL SALOON
37. GUNDOWN IN PARADISE
38. KING OF THE BORDER
39. THE EL PASO SALT WAR
40. THE TEN PINES KILLER
41. HELL WITH A PISTOL
42. THE WYOMING CATTLE KILL
43. THE GOLDEN HORSEMAN
44. THE SCARLET GUN
45. NAVAHO DEVIL
46. WILD BILL'S GHOST

And coming next month:
THE GUNSMITH #48: ARCHER'S REVENGE

THE GUNSMITH
47
THE MINERS' SHOWDOWN

J.R. ROBERTS

CHARTER BOOKS, NEW YORK

THE GUNSMITH #47: THE MINERS' SHOWDOWN

A Charter Book/published by arrangement with
the author

PRINTING HISTORY
Charter edition/December 1985

All rights reserved.
Copyright © 1985 by Robert J. Randisi
This book may not be reproduced in whole
or in part, by mimeograph or any other means,
without permission. For information address:
The Berkley Publishing Group, 200 Madison Avenue,
New York, New York 10016.

ISBN: 0-441-30951-8

Charter Books are published by The Berkley Publishing Group,
200 Madison Avenue, New York, New York 10016.
PRINTED IN THE UNITED STATES OF AMERICA

ONE

It had been years since the Gunsmith had visited the mountain paradise of Lake Tahoe, but he never forgot its great beauty. And now as he unsaddled his magnificent black gelding, Duke, and turned him out to graze in the lush forest meadow, Clint Adams figured he and Duke were long overdue for a peaceful vacation.

They had ridden and faced danger all across the west and both of them had the scars to prove it. Clint had standing invitations for a warm bed and good food from dozens of lovely and exciting women, but he figured that sometimes a man needed to get an uninterrupted, full night's sleep. Besides, there were periods in life when it was good to go off alone and be left in peace—when he could go to bed when he wanted, get up when he felt like it, then do nothing at all but relax and enjoy the day as it unfolded without worrying about someone else.

Hard riding and long hours in the saddle had left both Clint and Duke far too lean, and he was going to remedy that by letting his horse get fat on meadow grass while he caught some big speckled trout out of this clear, cold lake. An old man had once shown Clint the finer points of catching fish and told him that the colder the water, the better the meat. If that were true, Clint guessed the trout in this lake would taste mighty good. There were deer and mountain sage hens, too, that he could hunt so that he didn't become jaded on trout.

Clint wasn't used to a fancy camp. Normally, all he carried was his bedroll, a change of clothes, a frying pan, a coffee pot, and a few provisions for the trail. When he wasn't settled and practicing the craft of gunsmithing, he was a man who believed in traveling light.

But for this long-awaited vacation, he'd really indulged himself. He'd bought a new canvas tent, one big enough to eat in if it rained, a folding chair and table, an oil lantern, and plenty of California wine and good Kentucky whiskey. He'd also bought a very expensive fishing pole and reel along with plenty of tackle and about a half dozen books he'd never seemed to find the time to read.

Clint set about erecting the tent, blushing a little at all the fancy gear he'd brought and glad that some of his rougher male friends weren't around to discover the side of him that enjoyed luxury and creature comforts—a side that only his ladies ever got to see. It took him almost an hour to erect the tent, but it was worth it, and he carefully set the guy ropes and anchored them solidly with stakes so that even in the heaviest wind the tent would hold solid and not blow away into the pine trees.

He put his new folding table and chairs just outside the door and then gathered loads of pine needles and used them to form a mattress over which he stretched his bedroll. When he tested it out, it was as soft as the best mattress in San Francisco.

Finally, he neatly stacked his provisions near the tent and then stood back to survey his new camp with no small measure of pride. This was going to be the most enjoyable month of his life. He took a deep breath and filled his lungs with the sharp, pine-scented mountain air. Overhead, a pair of bluejays were giving each other hell, but when he clapped his hands and scared them away, the mountain was silent and serene.

Clint rigged his fishing pole and spent less than ten minutes in the grassy meadow digging up some fat earthworms. Then, whistling a tune, he moseyed down to the blue sapphire that was Lake Tahoe.

The water was incredibly clear; Clint could see rocks a good fifty feet under the surface and they seemed magnified. He watched fish as long as his forearm swimming in lazy circles, and he settled down on a big rock, eagerly baited his hook, and tossed it wriggling into the lake. The worm sank slowly, it spun around and around, and then, suddenly, out of the depths of the lake, a huge trout appeared to gobble it up with one bite.

Clint laughed with delight and then began to play the fish for all it was worth. It was a whopper! At least twenty inches long, he thought, it fought like a whale, and he let it battle itself out, enjoying the fight immensely. When he pulled the trout up onto the big rock that he'd chosen to fish upon, he grabbed it under the gills and deftly removed the hook and then measured the fish.

"You're a shade smaller than I first thought," he said, judging it to be only about sixteen inches. "I'm going to throw you back and hold out for a granddaddy."

He pitched the fish back and it fell down to the water below and then swam away fast. Hell, the best part of fishing was catching them anyway! Clint rebaited his hook and cast out from the rock. The lake rippled softly and the trees framed the water like a picture. It was going to be a real nice day.

One hour and at least a dozen fish later, Clint hooked up with a monster that fought him for almost ten minutes before he could swing it up on the rock. "Boy are you a beauty!" he said with a low whistle of appreciation. He removed the hook and admired the fish's beautiful speckles and pink coloring. He held it up against the slate-blue Sierra sky. It was at least two feet long.

And that's the way he was, just standing on a cabin-size rock holding a trophy-size fish when the first bullet shattered the mountain solitude. Clint pivoted around, one hand going for his gun that, he discovered, he'd left back at camp. Out of the forest burst a young woman riding for her very life and then, even as Clint lost his balance and the trout flipped loose to regain its freedom, he saw three more riders appear. Just as the riders opened fire on the woman, he windmilled his arms frantically to keep from toppling into the lake.

Clint swore hopelessly as his boots slid on the rock and he began to lean out over the water. He saw the woman rein her horse toward his camp and drive it over his guy ropes so that the stakes went flying. So did her horse. Then the tent itself twisted up into the air and the girl did a complete somersault, landing on his new table and smashing it to smithereens.

He was falling. "Hey!" he yelled as the girl struggled to rise, "you..." he was going to tell the three that they couldn't gun a woman down, but the icy waters of Lake Tahoe drowned his warning and took his breath away.

TWO

The numbing shock of impact and immersion doubled up Clint's body like a kick in the groin and his heart seemed to fill his throat. His breath exploded from his mouth and he clawed toward the surface, gasping and cursing. He cursed the girl who'd brought this storm of trouble in her wake and had driven her horse through his camp and destroyed his tent and table—cursed, too, the likes of three men who would be so vicious as to chase down a woman and attempt to take her life—and finally, cursed himself for leaving his gun at camp because he figured no one would ever find or disturb him in this isolated, peaceful wilderness.

Clint grabbed a mossy rock and dragged himself out of the water, spitting and fighting mad. He jumped to his feet and sloshed along the water's edge to see the three gunmen piling off their horses to surround the fallen woman.

"Stop!" he shouted in anger.

The three twisted around and did what he whould have guessed they'd do—they opened fire on him. Clint heard the bullets whip-cracking past his face and realized he was either going to get shot right then and there or he was going back into the damned freezing lake. Neither choice was one bit appealing, but, of the two, he guessed he'd rather take another dive.

As the trio raced toward him firing their guns, Clint saw the young woman take advantage of the momentary distraction to jump up and bolt into the trees.

"She's getting away!" one of them screamed. "She's getting away!"

They milled in confusion. Then, seeming to reach a decision, two of them wheeled around and charged into the forest after the woman—that was the good part. She was young and looked to be built for speed, fast as a deer, and Clint figured she had at least some chance of escape—the bad part was that the third man was coming after him.

Clint swung around to face those numbing waters again and nothing but a bullet in the back would have forced him back in, yet when a shot plucked at the coat he wore, Clint sprang back into the lake and swam for his life. The lake was bordered by huge rocks like the one he'd been fishing from and he knew his only chance for survival was to find some underwater passage where he could reach a hidden cave.

He was a strong swimmer, but his water-filled boots and heavy leather jacket were dragging him down, making it impossible to swim effectively. Furthermore, Clint's lungs were already starting to burn for oxygen. He looked up at the glassy surface. He thought he was about ten feet under and then he worked his way to the green underbelly of a boulder and forced himself to rise slowly. There was just no way of knowing whether anyone would be waiting to kill him the moment he surfaced.

Clint was wild for fresh air now. The lack of it was bleeding the strength from his arms and legs as if someone had sliced his arteries. His hands clawed upward along the mossy rock and then, with the last of his control, he broke the surface with little more than a ripple and somehow quietly emptied his throbbing lungs and refilled them with life-giving air.

He pressed his face to the rock and tried to catch his breath, tried to clear the haze that had begun to cloud his eyes and his mind. His lungs bellowed gratefully and he tried to think again with clarity. If I could...

A trickle of gravel rained down from overhead and told him that a gunman was almost directly above him, probably working his way around for a clear shot. Clint swore silently and measured the shoreline. He had to get away from this man and somehow return to his camp and arm himself. Then he'd see about swinging the odds in his favor. Hell, three woman-shooters didn't seem like too much of a match for the Gunsmith!

He saw the man's hat poke out into the blue sky. If Clint had six-foot arms, he might have been able to grab the murderous son of a bitch and drag him screaming into the water. But his arms weren't nearly that long and he knew that the gunman would kill him for sure if he stayed where he was.

After tearing off his leather jacket and custom-made boots, he reluctantly let them sink before he took a deep breath and followed them down. Now he could really swim and his arms and legs pumped powerfully as he moved under and around the clutter of boulders and sunken logs. He was searching for that hiding place where he could remain out of view until it was safe to come out, retrieve his gun, and attack. Most men would have just wanted to hide, to wait out the last hours of the day and slip away under the protective cover of nightfall. But not the Gunsmith. Hiding from danger wasn't in his nature and neither was running. Three gunmen had invaded his camp and maybe killed a defenseless woman, and Clint wanted to nail their bullet-riddled hides to a pine tree before this day was ended. If he could save the woman, that would be all the better. So, even if the gunman who searched the water was sure he was the hunter, Clint figured the exact opposite would soon be the truth. He wasn't going to wait for dark; he was going to get the hell out of this freezing lake and go after them!

He had found a narrow crevice in the rocks and now, as he climbed out of the lake shivering in semidarkness, he could hear the man above searching—see his shadow poking out over the water.

Clint looked up at the slice of cobalt sky and slowly began

to inch his way up through the storm-wedged driftwood along a fissure. Another fifteen minutes in the water and he'd have been too numb to climb out. His body was already chilled to the marrow, his teeth wanted to rattle, and his hands and feet were as unfeeling as chunks of ice. He knew that, when the moment came to spring into action, he had to be ready because he'd only have one chance. If he stumbled, or made a warning sound, he'd be caught flat-footed and gunned down without having a fighting chance.

He picked his way up through the crevice, straining to hear the man overhead. Once, he tried to pull himself up and the limb he'd grabbed broke. Fortunately, its fiber was rotted and did not snap, but instead almost crumbled in his fist.

The crevice was not more than two feet wide, a fissure that split a great rock. Clint reached the top of it and took a deep, steadying breath. He prayed the gunman would not be waiting for his head to pop up so that he could blow it off.

He lifted his eyes and saw his man not ten feet away, squatted down on the heels of his boots, and leaning way out over the water, vainly searching for Clint.

It was now or never. Clint heaved his shivering body up onto the rock and came at the gunman in a soggy rush. The man heard the slosh of water. He reared back and twisted around but Clint was on him—grabbing his wrist even as the gun exploded almost pointblank in his face.

Clint was a wild man. He drew back his fist and sent it crashing against the man's jaw. He ripped the gun from his hand, breaking the man's finger and then using the weapon to smash him in the face.

"Help!"

Clint hurled him kicking and screaming off the rock to splash into the lake. He disappeared for a moment even as Clint twisted around to see the other two charging toward him from the direction of his demolished camp. Right then either panic or inexperience would have caused most men to open a return fire. But not the Gunsmith. He hadn't time to check but he figured he had just two, maybe three bullets remaining in the cylinder. He'd have to make each of them count dearly.

Clint flattened against the rock. He laid the pistol's barrel flat across his left forearm and tried to ignore the bullets whining off the granite beside him. He could hear the man he'd just fought shouting for help because he was obviously drowning.

He took a deep, steadying breath. One of the pair was a lot faster runner than his friend. He was a fool as well, wildly unleashing a hail of bullets as if his gun would never empty itself. Clint tried to stop shivering so that the gun in his fist steadied. He pressed its barrel harder against his own flesh and then, when the one in front was out of bullets and just now realizing his own danger, Clint drilled him through the buttons, knocked him flat over backward so that he landed and then didn't even twitch.

"Come on," Clint whispered softly to the last gunman, "I'm ready!"

But while the man was slower afoot, he was a whole lot more intelligent. When he saw how cleanly the Gunsmith had dropped his companion, he dived for cover and fired twice. Then, as Clint's last bullet slammed into his arm, he cried out in pain and took off running for his life.

As he swayed to his feet, Clint realized he was too exhausted by swimming and the cold to think he could outrun anyone. He glanced over the edge of the rock down at the water to see the first gunman floating face down. Drowning was not a good way to die but Clint guessed that the dead man got what he deserved.

He turned around and spun the cylinder of the revolver. Empty. He stood up, cold and shaking violently, to see the wounded man flogging the hell out of his mount as he galloped across the meadow to vanish in the trees, heading east in the direction of Nevada.

Clint shoved the empty gun into his backpocket and started toward what was left of his camp. The forest, just moments before ringing with gunfire, was now silent again and Clint wondered if he would soon find the body of a very pretty but also very dead young lady.

He sure as hell hoped not.

THREE

His camp was a wreck, table and chair flattened, provisions scattered over the ground, tent trampled by horses and men. All of this he noted with a glance, yet he didn't even break stride until he'd uncovered his bedroll and dug out his gun and holster. Sure, it was like closing the barn door after the horses got out, but he wasn't going to make the same mistake twice. That was the last time he'd allow himself to get caught unarmed.

The forest was quiet and he figured he'd better go search for the woman. This was hard and rugged country. The last time he'd seen her she was on foot and running for her life—probably scared out of her wits, helpless and crying, if she were still alive.

"Hello!" Clint shouted, stepping into the trees where she'd disappeared. "It's safe to come out now!"

His words echoed in the huge volcanic bowl that formed Lake Tahoe. Clint scrubbed his lean jaw and guessed there was nothing to do but go search for her. It was going to be dark soon and he'd be forced to give it up until morning if he didn't locate her fast. There were bears and mountain lions in this neck of the woods, and darkness under the pines would be like staggering around in an underground cavern.

He entered the forest and began to hunt, calling out every quarter of a mile and watching the light fade through the canopy of overhanging branches. Clint saw a few signs, but they were mostly those of the ones who'd searched for the woman. From the look of the tracks, how they kept circling and doubling back, Clint could see that they apparently didn't have any more luck tracking someone across a carpet of pine needles than he was having.

"Hello!" Clint cupped his hands together and shouted. "If you can hear me, I'm a friend. I'm trying to help you. I killed two of them, but the third one got away. You must need help. Can you hear me?"

Again, the echoing into silence.

Clint frowned. It was almost dark and he might get lost in this heavy forest if he didn't get back to his camp. Besides, he'd need time to put the damned tent back up and restore order. Maybe she was halfway to Sacramento by now or had friends up here somewhere.

"To hell with it," Clint grumbled, thinking about how a man would probably have to go camp in the center of a thousand square miles of sandhills before he could be certain he'd be left alone and in peace.

It was almost sundown when he stepped out of the forest and peered across the meadow to see the young woman pitching her saddle over his pack horse and frantically yanking on the cinch.

"Hey! What . . . hey, you can't steal my horse and saddle!"

She obviously had a different point of view. He saw her turn around and stare at him more in defiance than fear. She was tall and shapely, her hair was blond and disheveled, and even at a distance, he could see a nasty bruise on one pretty cheek.

"Stop it!" He shouted as he began to run. "I saved your life!"

The woman yanked the cinch tight and jammed her foot into the stirrup. She swung up onto the pack horse, sawed on the reins, then drummed her heels against the animal's ribs, and pointed it east.

"Damn!" he swore. He whistled for Duke, who threw his head up, and then came galloping across the meadow even as the woman vanished through the trees. Clint grabbed a fistful of the big horse's mane and swung onto its back. Guiding the animal with pressure from his knees, he sent it racing after the shapely horse thief.

Duke just laid back his ears and flat ate up the ground with his strong, fluid stride. When they shot into the forest, Clint was reminded of a train rushing into a long, black tunnel. He trusted Duke with his life and knew the great horse would run down the pack animal and safely guide him over or around fallen trees, rotting stumps, and whatever other obstacles they might find in their path.

It took Duke less than a mile to overtake the packhorse. "Stop, damn it!" Clint bellowed as they thundered along the narrow, winding forest trail.

When the woman looked back over her shoulder and saw him gaining with every stride, she reached down and began to pull out his Winchester rifle from its saddleboot.

Clint had seen enough! Not only was she an ungrateful horse thief, she was also ready to kill him! He flattened out on Duke's back until the gelding slowed and was running stride for stride with the smaller pack horse. Then, as she drew out the rifle and swung it around, Clint reached out and grabbed a fistful of her coat.

"Rein in!" he shouted, knocking the rifle out of her hands.

The woman wasn't ready to obey anyone. She reined away sharply and there was no way that Clint could hang on without leaving Duke. So he jumped and, together, he and the woman went crashing through a rotting log.

The impact momentarily stunned him. Clint groaned and finally rolled to his knees. A million termites were crawling over him and he almost went crazy as he brushed himself furiously, then came to his feet swaying with dizziness. At least no arms or legs were broken.

In the last light of day, he walked to the woman, who lay face down and unmoving. He bent and turned her over, half expecting she was faking and would try to gouge out his eyes. And if, after all the rest, she tried that, he was going to...

She wasn't faking. The girl was out cold and it took him only a minute to examine her head to feel the rising lump.

Clint stood up and whistled for Duke who came trotting back, the pack horse ambling along behind. Horses usually did like to keep each other company, especially in the mountains where there might still be a few bears roaming about at night.

He lifted her into the saddle, then climbed up behind the cantle, and held her upright while he reined the pack horse back toward camp. One thing for sure, he wasn't about to trust this wildcat in the dark. Nope. If she woke up in the night screaming and spitting and raising hell about the way her head ached and her hands and feet were tied, then that was just too bad.

He'd tell her to keep quiet so that he could get some sleep and they'd go over everything in the morning. The Gunsmith figured she owed him two things—an apology and an explanation. She had destroyed his peace and solitude, his camp, had almost got him shot, and had tried to steal his horse, saddle, and rifle—a rifle she'd tried to kill him with. If she were a man, he would have seriously considered stretching her neck from the limb of one of the big pines.

But she was a woman—a lot of woman by the feel of her. And that made things altogether different.

FOUR

In the morning he awoke early to find her sleeping. He'd gotten up in the night and had to stuff her mouth with his bandanna because she'd been yelling in anger and he was tired and in no mood for listening to anyone. He had, however, given her most of his blankets, and after being certain she could not reach a gun to kill him with, he'd gone back to sleep.

But now as he studied her by firelight, he suddenly remembered his fishing pole and the trout he'd pitched back into the lake. He felt a twinge of pity. Partly, he decided, it was because he never could hold a grudge against a pretty woman when she was asleep. Besides, this one with the bruise on her cheek and knot on the back of her head had obviously been through a lot of grief and it was a small wonder she was even alive.

Clint poured himself a cup of strong coffee and stretched painfully; that fall last night had left him a little banged up himself. This morning he'd put his tent back up and repair the table and chair. He still had one of the world's prettiest campsites and he meant to take up where he left off—once he decided what to do with the woman.

He was on his second cup of coffee and wondering if he could retrieve his coat, boots, and most importantly his pole and reel without going back into the lake when the woman awoke with a sudden start. Her dark blue eyes flew open and she began to struggle furiously at her bonds.

Clint forced a smile as he poured her a cup of coffee. "Miss, you might as well simmer down and drink the coffee I made. I'm not going to hurt you and I'm damn sure not letting you go free until I get a reasonable explanation as to why you've almost wrecked the first good vacation I've taken in the last fifteen years."

She was giving him hell. With her mouth stuffed with his bandanna, he couldn't understand her and that was just fine and dandy as far as he was concerned. Her face grew red and finally she ran out of steam and got quiet.

Clint walked over and squatted down beside her. "Miss, I did save your life," he said, looking right into the steel of her eyes. "I'm not one of them fellas chasing you if that's what's still on your mind. I'm just a man who likes to mind his own damn business until someone tries to push me around or spoil my day."

He took a sip of coffee. It was still damn near boiling. "Miss, before I take the gag out of your mouth and you yell something neither one of us wants to hear, I just want to say that I don't want or need anything from you except an explanation and an apology—and I don't care in which order they are given. Do you understand me?"

Her eyes finally softened and that made them very pretty again. She nodded. He took out the gag and then untied her wrists but left her ankles bound together just in case.

She took the coffee he offered and looked down at her tied ankles. "You're not a very trusting man," she told him, sipping the steaming coffee that immediately brought color back to her pale cheeks.

When she looked back at him, there was even the hint of a smile on her full lips. "I do apologize," she began. "You see, I didn't have time even to see their faces yesterday when they jumped my trail and opened fire."

"Do you know them?"

"I can guess. They're men hired by the Sutro Mining Corporation over on the Comstock Lode. They were sent to keep me from returning to Nevada. It was their plan to rob and then kill me."

"For what?"

She hesitated, ignored the question, and then countered with one of her own. "Who are you?"

"My name is Clint Adams."

"And you just..." she glanced around, "just came up here to relax and enjoy the scenery?" By her expression, it was clear she did not completely believe him.

"Yeah, and fish. Me and Duke deserved a change of pace and a good rest. I thought we'd found it here—until you and your friends arrived."

"You killed the three who were after me?"

He shrugged. "Actually, I just shot one dead. I knocked another into the lake and he drowned. The third man I wounded and he escaped. Who are you?"

She finished her coffee and he poured her a second cup. She sipped it, not seeming to mind that it was scalding hot. She looked fragile and delicate but she definitely was not.

"My name is Tessa O'Grady and I am on my way from Sacramento back to Virginia City to take rightful possession of the Shamrock Mine. It was owned by my dear father until they killed him two weeks ago."

"The Sutro Mining Corporation?"

"Who else? Haven't you ever heard of them?"

"No."

"Figures. King Cleaver runs that corporation and avoids publicity like it was the plague. But he's going to try to take the Comstock over. The man is totally ruthless."

Clint had spent years wearing a sheriff's badge, and he knew that accusations were cheap without facts. "Do you have any proof they killed your father?"

"Of course not! If there were any witnesses, they'd be dead and at the bottom of some worthless mine shaft by now. But it was King and his hired guns all right. And they want my Shamrock Mine."

She rolled over on one side and pulled a folded document out of her hip pocket. "I've no choice but to trust you, Mister..."

"Clint. Clint Adams."

"Clint. Here. Take a look and see if I'm not telling you the truth. My father must have known he was going to be murdered and somehow, he had this deed and the letter with it sent to me at the very last moment. You read them and you'll understand that I'm telling you the truth."

Clint read both the deed and the letter and it pretty well proved that Tessa wasn't lying. The deed was official and the letter had a desperate tone to it, the kind a man who figured he was about to die would use. Handwritten in a barely legible scrawl, it told how he'd already been shot at twice from ambush and probably would be again.

"Clint?"

He looked up.

"If you help me, I'll give you half the gold we mine out of that claim. Half of it! My father knew it was worth a fortune and so does King Cleaver and his corporation or they wouldn't be so damn eager to get it."

What she was saying sounded true and plenty logical but Clint still wasn't interested. "I'm no miner, Tessa, and I don't want half interest. I've been in a few of them and they give me a hard, closed-in feeling. Besides, I wouldn't know the first thing about what to look for."

"Neither would I but father was sure the mine shaft he was working was leading right to a fortune. I'm telling you, Clint, in a few weeks, months at the longest, we could both be millionaires!"

He had to admit to the temptation, but still, this was his vacation and he was tired as hell. "No, thanks," he said quietly.

She set her coffee cup down. "Clint, I must have your help. You're exactly the kind of man who can stand up to Cleaver and his bunch of killers and help me find that gold."

"How do you know I'm your man?" he asked. "You don't know one thing about me."

"Oh, yes, I do. You're a gunfighter, aren't you?"

Clint shook his head. "I'm a gunsmith by trade."

"Bullshit!" She sighed. "Didn't mean to swear at you but gunsmiths don't handle themselves the way you did yesterday. No, you're definitely not just a common gunsmith. You are a man who is used to trouble and who can handle anything that comes his way. Isn't that true?"

"I was a lawman for many years," he conceded matter-of-factly. "I have had to kill a few men who needed killing, but that's all in the past now."

"Is it? I don't think a man like you could ever settle down to something routine. Besides," she added, "you'd have to work a thousand years to earn a million dollars."

"Money isn't all that important to me," he said, wondering what it would be like to be a millionaire, even for just a day or two.

Tessa studied him carefully. Her blue eyes covered the length of him and must have liked what she saw because, without warning, she unbuttoned her blouse and drew it back from her shoulders.

Clint gasped quietly in surprise and admiration. Her breasts were as big and full as melons and probably a whole lot sweeter.

Tessa O'Grady winked like a vixen. "Maybe I can think of something in addition to a gold mine to attract your interest."

He chuckled with appreciation. "You are getting warmer, Tessa. But I still won't take on mining. I mean to have a vacation."

She was not a woman to give up easily. "That gold has been in the ground a long, long time. I guess it can wait a week or two longer for us. Now, why don't you untie my legs so we can start enjoying our holiday together."

Clint found the idea too hard to resist. He hadn't had any breakfast yet, but there was another kind of hunger that now seemed more important. He moved toward Tessa, unable to take his eyes off those gorgeous breasts with the already hardened nipples.

And deep in his loins, he could feel the fever of desire, a desire stronger than common, everyday gold fever. What the hell, seeing Tessa like this made him realize he hadn't wanted to be alone a whole month without a pretty woman, and sleeping or even fishing all day could get to be real boring. Yes, this was going to be an even finer vacation than he'd imagined.

FIVE

Tessa O'Grady was twenty-three and no virgin, but neither was she worldly. She'd had a few boyfriends and they'd rudely taught her the basics of making love. But most of them had been slobbering young men, hard and eager and wanting all pleasure—but too selfish to give any in return.

Tessa had heard that there were men who gave as well or better than they received and that was the kind of man she'd been looking for. And for some reason, this Clint Adams seemed exactly like the kind who might enjoy pleasuring a woman, teaching her how to reach the orgasm she'd heard about, yet had never felt.

Her voice was a little shaky, a little throaty as she watched him untie her ankles. "You've probably had more women than you've killed men, haven't you."

"Lots more, I'm happy to say." He finished the untying and took her by the shoulders and she closed her eyes as they kissed. At first, his lips were surprisingly soft against her own, but then they soon grew more insistent and she could feel her own heart begin to race as his hands came up to stoke her

THE MINERS' SHOWDOWN 21

breasts lightly. He took her nipples and rolled them gently between his thumb and forefinger and the sensation was enough to bring a slow warmth that quickly grew hotter down between her legs. Tessa tasted his mouth, felt his tongue against her own, and she wriggled with excitement.

He tore his lips from hers and she knew a moment of disappointment that quickly was forgotten as he lowered his mouth to a hard nipple and began to circle it with his wet, rough tongue.

"Oh, yes, Clint," she breathed raggedly. "Show me what a man can do for a woman."

His mouth closed over her breast and she gasped with pleasure as he began to suck. He started to unsnap her riding pants. She wriggled her hips to help him free her of the pants and then her panties. The mountain air felt cool on her exposed thighs and she had a passing moment when she wondered if anyone else might come bursting into this camp.

"The other one," she whispered, "suck the other one."

He obliged her and she began to squeeze her breasts together so that he could take both of her aching nipples between his lips and stroke them with his tongue.

Tessa closed her eyes and her head swam with pleasure. Already he was giving her more than any of the other hot, sweaty, rutting young roosters she'd given herself to.

He tore his mouth away and gazed at her with such unconcealed lust and admiration that she blushed with pride and pleasure. "Like what you see, Clint?" she asked, knowing damn well that he did. He was looking her over as if she were a Thanksgiving turkey he was about to eat.

"Want to go inside my tent?" he asked.

"Wouldn't we have to rig it up first."

"Yep," he said with a boyish grin. "And that would take a little while but what I'm about to do to you might be a little unnerving for a young woman out in the open.

She took a deep breath. "I've got plenty of nerve, Clint. Do to me what you want. But just forget the tent and start now!"

He didn't need instructing. His mouth began to work its way following the soft, golden hairs of her belly down until her fingers were pulling his face lower and lower, and then she stiffened and moaned, threw her long shapely legs outward, and guided his mouth and his tongue into her womanhood. Her head rolled back on her shoulders and she groaned with a hunger she'd never known before.

"Oh, Clint, yes, don't stop, don't even slow down!"

She felt him pull back for a moment and laugh in a nice, easy way. She began to rotate her hips.

He was driving her crazy! He had her by the core, his teeth were nipping softly at her, and Tessa forgot all about being under control as her hips began to bounce and pump and grind uncontrollably. "Do it! Do it harder!"

She grabbed him by the back of the head. Wave after wave of pleasure beat at her senses until one giant one seemed to sweep over her. Then she was falling back and screaming in ecstasy. Her beautiful legs were waving like branches and his fingers were digging into the flesh of her round and shuddering buttocks.

Tessa lay back on the pine needles and felt as if something inside of her had been released in a flood of pleasure that she'd never even known could exist. She was trembling like a leaf and could not seem to keep her hips still as they slowly rotated under the man who now licked her softly, took her down gently.

She licked her lips and pulled him up on top of her and her eyes were shining with gratitude and joy. "I can't beleive what you did to me, Clint. It was a fire coming up through my body pulling me apart and yet I never wanted it to stop."

"It will get even better before we leave," he vowed.

She smiled, but shook her head. "That's impossible." But on second thought, she believed him. "Now, I want to return the favor."

Tessa had never taken a man into her mouth before, but she knew she wanted this one. He had given her more than she'd ever had, given freely and happily, and she was going to do the same for him before he filled her with his seed.

She swallowed dryly and sat up, gently pushing him down as she began to unbutton his shirt, then his pants. When she pulled away to reveal his fully erect member, she took a deep breath because it was far larger than any she'd seen before.

"It doesn't bite," he said looking up at her. "But if I'm the first man you have ever done this to, I'll be a little more careful."

"You do what comes natural, Clint. And you tell me what feels good or not so good."

He ran his strong hands into her long, blond hair and nodded. "It'll all feel good, Tessa, so no more talking."

He drew her face down. She opened her lips, and her tongue darted out to sweep across the head of his cock, and she heard him suck in his breath a little. That encouraged her, gave her more confidence, and she opened her mouth and slowly took him inside, rolling her tongue around and around until his hips were jerking up and down with passion and he was moving her face down even harder.

Tessa looked up at him, saw the glassy pleasure in his eyes, and knew that she was doing just fine. She took as much of him into her mouth as she could and began to work up and down on him.

"You have a natural talent," he moaned.

Tessa sucked faster, enjoying what she was doing to this man. He was strong and handsome and loving, and she felt happy that she could capture him in her mouth and give him everything he wanted just as he'd done to her.

"That's enough!" he cried.

She raised her head, "Why, can't you stand it anymore?"

"You learn much too fast." He was nearly out of breath.

She then grabbed his slick, engorged cock and raised her hips, straining to pull him into her. His pubic hair was coal black, thick as a rug; hers was soft and silken and blond. She wanted to see those colors blending, then mixing together.

He let the head of his cock nudge past the lips and go into her, then he stiffened with resistance. Her buttocks moved eagerly, for she was frantic to pull this man completely inside of her.

Only then did he thrust deeply into her until she thought he was going to drive himself clear through her.

For a moment, she just lay still as if impaled. And then, she reached and grabbed both of his muscular cheeks. He took control of her from the first grind of his hips to the very last.

He pumped her, pumped with her until the flesh between her thighs was burning and she was yelling and bucking out of control. He pumped her until she begged him to go, to explode deep inside of her and quench the raging fire within. Still he would not stop until they both were tearing at each other, working like pistons and driving themselves wildly, desperately.

Tessa lost control completely. She dimly realized that she was milking him and that he was driving into her. Suddenly, he was unleashing a torrent way up inside of her even as she felt another orgasm blossoming. She cried out until they were both gasping and quivering in each other's arms.

SIX

Clint finished burying the two men and wiped the dirt from his hands. He had first supposed the thing to do was to take their bodies down to Reno, give them to the sheriff, and answer a whole lot of questions while some overworked and underpaid deputy filled out a half dozen forms. Then, a money-hungry undertaker would demand that someone pay for their burial and Clint figured it would wind up being him.

So he and Tessa just buried the pair in the meadow without a marker and let it go at that. Afterward, she helped him erect the tent. It was all done by midmorning and he was limping around barefooted and wondering if there was any chance of retrieving his boots and jacket from the lake.

They moved down to the lakefront and climbed the rocks where he'd fallen. She knelt down and studied the water carefully.

"I can see it, Clint! Your fishing pole is down there on the sandy bottom."

He frowned. He had to have that pole back if they were going to stay any time at all. He'd need it to catch fish.

"Guess there's no help for it," he grumbled, unbuttoning his shirt with dread.

"You wait right here," Tessa said, pulling off her blouse and then shucking out of her pants.

Clint didn't argue with her. In fact, it was all he could do to keep from grabbing the woman and making love to her again on the sun-warmed rock.

"You don't have any idea how cold that water is," he warned.

"Maybe not, but I'm about to find out." Tessa brushed back her long blond hair and made a graceful dive. Her body cut through the surface of the lake with barely a ripple and it was a damn pretty sight the way her sleek, white body flowed down through the water.

Clint saw her knife downward and keep going until she was just a white blur in the depths of the lake. He grew anxious when he saw a small cloud of air bubbles come floating up.

"Come on!" he whispered anxiously. "Tessa!"

She wasn't coming and he wasn't waiting another second. Gritting his teeth against the shock he knew was coming, Clint dived into the water, and it wasn't any more pleasant the second time around than it was the first.

He swam furiously and, if anything, the water got even colder. She was ten feet below him when he saw her look up at him and wave. Then, as if she had all the time in the world, she pulled his fishing pole out of the sand and came swimming up just like some mermaid—only the bottom half of her sure wasn't any fish.

When they broke the surface, he was already needing fresh air and he was also madder than hell. Tessa took a deep breath and then raised his fishing pole up to the sky.

"Got it, Clint!"

"What took you so long!" he demanded.

"Your fishing hook and line was all tangled in a branch down there. I had to untangle it."

He stared at her in amazement. "You mean you stayed down there all that time just to save a fishing hook?" He couldn't believe his own ears.

She swam to a low rock and set his pole down on it, then turned around and motioned for him to come to her. She looked so fresh and happy he couldn't resist.

Tessa wrapped her arms around him, crowded him with those luscious breasts of hers, and rubbed the nipples against his chest. "Is this really that bad?" she asked.

He could feel himself getting hard, so he guessed it would be ridiculous to lie. Any woman who could do that to a man up to his neck in near freezing water had to be doing something right.

"I have a confession to make," she told him. "I didn't stay down that long just to save a hook. I knew you'd have plenty of them. I've been fishing before with my father."

"Then why did you stay down so long?"

"I wanted to see if you'd do something you really hated to do to save my life. I wanted to know that you'd do that for me, Clint. It was important. Now, I know I can trust you with anything and there is nothing I wouldn't do for you."

"What else could you give me?" he asked treading water and searching for the nearest flat rock that he could lay this woman down on.

"I can make us both rich. We could be the richest husband and wife team in Nevada."

Clint's smile dissolved in a hurry and he shook his head. "No strings, Tessa. I'm not interested in marriage. Not to anyone."

She hid her disappointment very well. Reaching out, she pulled his mouth to hers and kissed him hard. "But you are interested in this—and becoming a millionaire, aren't you?"

"What man wouldn't be?" he chuckled, pushing himself up and into her. "I bet very few men have done this in ice-cold water."

She closed her eyes and clung to him with her arms and her legs while he pushed her up against a barely submerged rock. "And I bet very few men even could."

Clint began to pump harder and harder, knowing full well he had to agree.

Afterward, they'd both dived to retrieve his jacket and expensive leather boots. Clint set the jacket out on the sunny meadow grass. He wore the boots until the leather dried and they were molded to his feet and fit better than they ever had before.

In between lovemaking, they spent wonderful days fishing and hiking or reading to each other from books. Days that unfolded like Tessa's hidden passion left them both filled and well satisfied.

Clint could have spent the entire summer up at Lake Tahoe and enjoyed every minute of it except for the knowledge of what lay waiting back at the Big Bonanza—better known as the Comstock Lode.

To her credit, Tessa never said another word about the Shamrock Mine or her eagerness to reclaim what was rightfully hers. Clint really appreciated that. He liked a woman who wasn't always pushing a man to do the next thing, never enjoying the present situation.

She was one hell of a woman. If he didn't go back to Virginia City, he knew she would go alone even though that meant she'd probably be murdered by this King Cleaver fella who ran the Sutro Mining Corporation. Clint just could not let that happen.

The idea of striking a house-size pocket of pure gold or silver and becoming a millionaire was exciting, but it wasn't what would take him back with her. And if they did strike it rich, he'd not be too proud to take some money for his services, but he wasn't going to take half the Shamrock Mine and make himself a rich man. The Gunsmith had seen dozens of good men go bad because of the chance for a quick fortune. A million dollars could turn anyone around in a hurry and tempt even a man of the cloth.

No, Clint thought, a man needed enough money to go where he wanted, when he wanted, to do what he wanted—but that didn't take being rich or having all the headaches that came with it. And if he had a good horse and good friends and was strong and healthy enough to enjoy a good woman like Tessa, what else was there in life?

Tessa finished frying him another trout and served it to him with a glass of cold, white California wine.

"Thank you," he said.

She nodded and then picked listlessly at her own plate.

THE MINERS' SHOWDOWN

"What's the matter, Tessa? Are you getting a little sick of speckled trout?"

"Maybe just a little."

He looked out into the forest. "Perhaps I ought to get around to going deer hunting. One good buck would take care of us for another couple of weeks."

"I guess it would," she said quietly.

He set his plate down and moved over to kneel beside her. "Actually, I'm getting a little tired of fish, too. And I can tell that Duke is fed up with meadow grass and is getting restless. Maybe it's about time we broke camp and got down to mining. You ready?"

In answer, she threw her arms around him and hugged his neck. "I'm just afraid of what will happen to you over there," she whispered. "The man that got away will recognize you, Clint. From the moment we ride in, you'll be a target."

"I've been a target all of my life and so I'm plenty used to it."

She pulled back to stare at him. "I've been thinking, Clint. Maybe you were right when you said money isn't all that important. Maybe we ought to just stay right here and forget the Shamrock. It was the cause of my father's death."

"And it could be the cause of ours," he told her thoughtfully. "But is that what you really believe? That people should play dead while men like this Cleaver fella and his big corporation just take whatever they want? Run roughshod and be allowed to rob and murder the little folks like your father?"

Her chin lifted defiantly. "No," she said, "that isn't what I believe at all. It's just that I'm a little bit..."

"Say it out loud, Tessa. You're a little scared at what's going to happen, aren't you?"

"Yes. Yes, I am."

"Well, I have to admit that I am, too," he said.

"You are?" She did not believe him.

"Sure. Only a fool wants to die when life is as good to him as this. And no matter how good I am with a gun, there is probably someone, somewhere, better. Besides, a fast gunhand is no defense for an ambusher's bullet."

"But you believe we have to go, don't you?"

"I do for all the reasons I just explained. Man or woman, they both have to do what they know is right. And going back and working your mine is right."

Tessa kissed him hard and pulled him down on her as her hands searched for the buckle of his pants.

"You are right! But it doesn't mean we can't put off leaving a few more hours, does it?"

He felt her soft hands bringing his manhood to a fast rise as he began to unbutton her blouse.

"No," he said happily, "it sure doesn't!"

SEVEN

They rode out of the Sierras down into the great Carson Valley of Nevada where the pines melted into grass and then to sage. Clint had been to Virginia City several times and figured it was about the most godawful country a man could find to put a town. The Comstock was up on the slopes of Sun Mountain, and in the summer it baked and in the winter it froze. There weren't any trees to speak of, just some scrubby juniper pines that weren't good for anything. Before the white man discovered ore here, the Paiute Indians had harvested the pinenuts each fall and used them for a large part of their winter food supply. But after the miners, they were cut down for firewood and for bracing the mines. Now the hills were bare except for the sage and Clint figured the trees might never come back to this part of the country.

He and Tessa passed through the little settlement of Genoa, once called Mormon Station because it was founded by those people back about the time of the California gold rush. It had prospered as a trading point where the forty-niners could buy new clothing, tobacco, meat, sardines, and fresh horses and mules to pull their wagons up and over the Sierras so that they could reach the diggings. The Mormons had built a fine town and some of the best farms and ranches in Nevada, but then Brigham Young had called them all back to Salt Lake City and the Mormons had been forced to practically give away their holdings. It was said that they cursed this valley with winds, and Clint guessed there might be something to that story because the wind blew hard and constant. It was called the Washoe zephyr.

They followed the Carson River, which was filled with logs and dotted with sawmills that ran day and night to keep the Comstock in shoring timber. "We'll ride up through Gold Hill Canyon," Clint said, reining Duke away from the river to the north. They began to climb into the low hills almost immediately.

"This is Gold Hill, Tess. Virginia City doesn't raise all the hell in these parts."

From the balcony of a two-story hotel, two pretty young women began to wave and shout excitedly. "Clint! It's Clint Adams!"

Tessa frowned. "I believe you have some fans up there," she said. "Why don't you tell them they'll have to wait to get paid after we strike it rich!"

He smiled and waved at the pair of women. "Candy, Monique, how have you been?"

"Lonely for you, Clint darlin', when you coming back to visit?" Candy responded.

"I don't know. Maybe after I strike it rich!"

They thought that was hilarious and blew kisses at him as he and Tessa rode on by.

Tessa wasn't amused at all. "You seem to attract women," she groused, "all the wrong kinds. They'll leave you with nothing, Clint."

The Gunsmith was offended by her implication. "I never have paid a woman for climbing into bed with me and I never will. Not even one that promises half a gold mine."

Her cheeks flamed. "Damn you for saying that! I don't need you or anyone else," she swore slapping her horse across the rump and galloping up the street.

Clint let her go ahead. She did need him and he was happy to help her out because he liked her and figured she deserved better than she'd get if she were alone. But still, he didn't want any woman ever to think she could lead him around by the nose because of love or money. He believed in giving as well as receiving—good or bad. He also figured some people were meant to plant roots and grow families and some weren't and that he was definitely one of the latter, at least at this point in his life.

He rode on alone through Gold Hill noticing how the little mining town had prospered since his last visit. The street was clogged with huge, high-sided ore wagons being pulled by long spans of mules and oxen. There were two new smelting plants and dozens of thriving businesses, most of which were saloons and whorehouses. Miners filled the narrow boardwalks, and piano and banjo music flowed into the streets. Most of the men looked overworked and unusually happy and drunk. That meant the big Comstock mines were doing well and that money was being made by everyone.

Just ahead he saw Devil's Gate, a point at which Gold Canyon pinched in so tightly that two wagons could barely squeeze through at the same time. There hadn't been much here the last time Clint had ridden through, but now there was an entire little settlement complete with its own hotel, barber shop, express office, brewery, saloon, and tollkeeper's station.

Tollkeeper's station? Clint frowned. This road had always been free to any man. Why should a man have to pay to travel a dirt road?

Tessa was stopped and arguing loudly with the tollkeeper. Clint put Duke into an easy gallop and rode up to find out what was wrong.

"Clint," she said angrily, "he wants three dollars from me!"

The man was big and heavyset. He had long black hair that ran out from under his hatband and a full beard with a lot of food and grease still stuck in it. A Winchester rifle in his fat hands pointed in Clint's direction.

Clint nodded with as much friendliness as he could muster. "All this is new, Mister," he said gesturing toward the hotel, saloon, and brewery, "you own it?"

"I do for a fact," the man rumbled. "What business is it of yours?"

"I suppose you expect me to pay, too?"

"Damn right."

"How much?" Clint's voice was easygoing. No one could have read the thoughts that were boiling in his mind. Thoughts that added up to the conclusion that he damned sure wasn't going to pay this man to ride between those towering rocks along a public road.

"Dollar for you."

Clint's eyebrows raised. "How come one dollar for me and three for the lady?"

The man smiled, cold and ugly. "I figure she might want to come inside my little hotel here and let me diddle her so she can pass for free."

Tessa's eyes flashed. "You filthy animal! I wouldn't let you touch me for a million dollars!"

The gatekeeper cursed and grabbed for her horse's bit. It was the distraction Clint had been looking for. He touched spurs to Duke and the big horse responded perfectly by leaping forward, slamming its shoulder into the man, and knocking him into the rock wall.

Clint's gun was out and was leveled down at the tollkeeper. "I ought to burn this place of yours down and run you out of this canyon."

Instead of cringing or begging Clint to show him mercy, the man climbed to his feet and snarled, "You must be a real fool. And you better climb down from that horse of yours and take your medicine right now."

Clint stared at the tollkeeper in amazement. "Maybe you have poor eyes," he said. "I'm the one holding the gun. Not you."

"You better look up above to the rocks and drop that gun or you and this woman are going to be visiting our new cemetery."

Both he and Tessa craned their heads up and now they saw two guards looking down the sights of their rifles at them. They were twenty feet overhead; there wasn't a chance in this world that they would miss. Clint dropped his gun to the dirt. To do anything else would have been suicidal.

"Now climb on down and let's see how well you do on your feet."

Tessa looked right at him and there was a lot of worry in her blue eyes. Justified, Clint thought.

The tollkeeper outweighed him by a good seventy-five pounds. And even if, by some stroke of luck, he did manage to whip this monster, what about the two guards up above?

Clint shrugged his shoulders. Up in Virginia City there was a whole pack of trouble waiting for Tessa and any man fool enough to help her—he was that fool and he'd like to have arrived there at least healthy and in one piece.

EIGHT

Clint did not enjoy fistfighting the way some men did. There was nothing amusing or pleasant about breaking someone's jaw or nose or getting his own face or knuckles broken. And there was another thing, a man with a reputation for being fast on the draw was always in danger of a challenge, and he certainly could not afford to have his hands battered and swollen.

But there were times, like this, when a man had absolutely no choice. This big son of a bitch liked to kick and stomp, gouge eyes, and bite off ears and noses; Clint had seen and fought the type and this man fit the bill right down the line. There was only one way to take on this kind of man and that was for Clint to be meaner, faster, rougher, and more savage than he was—otherwise, he'd maim and humiliate him.

"Maybe," Clint said, "we could talk this over and reach some kind of friendly agreement."

"You pulled a gun on me, your goddamn horse ran over the top of me, and your ladyfriend insulted me so the time for talking is over," the tollkeeper said, propping his rifle against the rock wall and spitting into the palms of his hands. "I'm gonna enjoy putting scars all over that nice face of yours."

THE MINERS' SHOWDOWN

Clint glanced up at the guards who had their rifles trained on him. "You boys got ringside seats," he said, noticing that if he got close enough to the rock wall only one of them would have a clear line of fire.

He looked at Tessa. He patted her horse and whispered, "If I win, you pile off and hit the wall. If I lose, ride like hell. Even these boys couldn't shoot a woman in the back."

"I hope you win."

There didn't seem to be much point in telling her he obviously felt the same way, so Clint moved from between their horses and set his mind to the task at hand. "Come and get it when you've a mind," he said, raising his fists.

The tollkeeper lifted his own fists and they were the size of hams. Big and scarred and knuckle-busted. Then, he waddled forward.

Clint feinted with his left and crossed with a right that thudded hard against the man's eye and rocked him back on his heels. He was jolted and surprised. "You can sting a little," he said, licking his lips.

"I can do more than that," Clint said, dancing back as a looping right stirred the air about where his own head would have been waiting.

Clint punched the man while he was off balance, hit him hard alongside the jaw, and spun him half around. Then he chopped a wicked overhand left that staggered him.

The man pushed off the rock wall and charged with a low, animal sound deep in his thick throat.

Clint tried to get out of the way, but the footing was rocky and he tripped. Then he felt the lights in his head almost go out as a fist connected with his own jaw hard enough to lift him completely off the ground. Before he could recover, the man was on him like a big old spider. He grabbed Clint around the waist, butted him in the forehead, and slammed him into the rock wall twice.

Clint went momentarily limp and the tollkeeper grunted with satisfaction, then buried his fingers in Clint's jacket and leaned him up against the rock wall and measured the finishing punch. Clint pretended to be dazed, but when the man's fist streaked in, he ducked.

"Agghhh!" the tollkeeper screamed, holding his ruined and bloody hand up.

The Gunsmith was still alive because in addition to being the best with a gun, he was also a man who had learned when to grab opportunity. His fist caught the man with his mouth wide open and yelling in agony. It sent him reeling and Clint moved in slamming blow after blow to that huge, pendulous belly—beating it like a bowl of raw eggs and making the tollkeeper suck and wheeze with each punishing blow. When the fat man's eyes rolled up to the guards and begged silently for help, Clint grabbed him and used him as a cover.

"You shoot and you kill the man who pays you!" he warned, yanking the man's pistol from his holster. "And even more important, I'll get both of you."

The guard directly above Clint had no shot but the other one did, and maybe it occurred to him that his rifle bullet probably had enough force to pass through the fat man's body and reach Clint. But that wasn't what he was hired to do and there was something about Clint's warning that told him he'd die, too.

"I could let you climb back on that horse and ride," the guard said, "but I'd lose my job if you don't pay."

"That's your problem," Clint gritted. "Throw down your rifles, both of you. Then pay up for us or your first shot will be your last."

"Who the hell are you?" the man above Clint raged. "Our boss ain't never been whipped."

"He's called the Gunsmith," Tessa yelled, her eyes shining with pride. "That ought to help you fools decide."

Clint wished she hadn't said that even though both men threw down their weapons and raised their hands. He'd have to have a talk with this woman—the last thing he needed was for every young fool who still dreamed of becoming a gunfighter and earning a fast reputation to learn that he was on the Comstock.

"Jesus, why didn't you just say so in the first place," the man swore. "None of us want no trouble with the likes of you."

Clint grabbed the fat man by the shirt, spun him around,

THE MINERS' SHOWDOWN

and slammed his head up against the rock wall twice just so he'd also know how it felt.

He let him spill into the dirt. "A man shouldn't have to give his name to anyone he doesn't want to and he damn sure shouldn't have to pay to travel up this canyon. If I ever come back this way again, you tell this fat boss man of yours he better be polite or I'll cut him down to size. You understand?"

He was out in the middle of the road now and his head hurt so bad it felt as if it had been used for a drum. But he was furious and it must have showed because the pair of guards disappeared fast.

"Well," Tessa said, her voice full of admiration, "you really are a hell of a man! But then, I knew that already."

He climbed unsteadily onto his horse and rode on through Devil's Gate. Clint rubbed his jaw and ran his finger across his teeth making sure they were all still there. He was thinking that this girl attracted trouble like flies to sugar candy. True, even if he were alone he would not have paid the toll, but he'd have drawn a gun and made the fat man call off his guards pronto, thus saving himself from having to fight.

Yep, he thought a little bleakly, she was trouble all right, but as his eyes slid over those long, shapely legs and the tempting swell of her full breasts, he thought that it was a trouble that also had its rewards.

Still and all, if she'd already caused him to have to kill two men, wound a third and then damn near get beaten silly, he could only imagine what might lay ahead in Virginia City. To his way of figuring, so far Tessa had only brought him fun and games.

The real trouble lay just over the Divide.

NINE

They had no trouble after that, and when they crossed the Divide, before them lay the famous Virginia City. It was a big, sprawling city with no less than four major blocks of downtown business clinging to the flanks of Sun Mountain. People said that there was not one thing in the biggest cities of the world that a man couldn't have here if he had the money. Clint guessed that was probably true. The Comstock had made millionaires out of men with names like Mackay, Fair, O'Brien, Flood, Hearst, and Ralston. Some of them had come and made fortunes, and then left as fast as they could take their money out of Nevada, but others had stayed and built fabulous mansions.

Clint had been invited into many of them, for a man with his reputation for danger always attracted those who had money but little real excitement. Clint had enjoyed visiting rooms where every stick of furniture was an imported European antique and a hand-carved French table might be worth more than a man earned in a lifetime. There were paintings by the master artists of Europe, and he'd admired them and learned something

THE MINERS' SHOWDOWN 41

about art and sculpture. Rich, oftentimes bored wives were only too happy to tell him all about their latest possessions and he was only too pleased to listen. They would have been astounded to know that the Gunsmith had a better understanding of European and old world cultures than they.

But art and money aside, Virginia City was what every boomtown in America dreamed of being—rich and bustling and powerful. Presidents, kings, queens, the most famous actors, and the most gifted orators all came to this city for one reason or another. And when they departed, they knew that they would never again see its equal in terms of raw power and vitality.

Clint stood up in his stirrups and surveyed the panorama that stretched out before him. "Well, Tessa, there it is. You may soon be counted among its overnight millionaires, but *we* may just as likely wind up in boot hill. You realize that, don't you? I'm good with a gun, but I can't guarantee that I can keep either one of us alive."

She nodded. "I'd be lying to you if I said that I wasn't afraid. But I'll never have a chance like this again. Maybe you won't either, Clint."

"That's true enough," he admitted. "Point out the Shamrock Mine."

"It's over there," she said. She dismounted, moved to the edge of a steep hillside, and pointed to the east. "Right next to the Golden Eagle Mine."

"I've heard that name mentioned a few times."

"You ought to have," Tessa said quietly, "it's one of the richest on the Comstock. It's worth millions and it has made King Cleaver most of his fortune. Does that tell you how valuable the Shamrock will be?"

"It sure does. Why don't you just sell it right now? Ought to bring you thousands of dollars even if it's no deeper than a grave."

"Because that's just what it would be for anyone foolish enough to buy it—a grave. Besides, there is one thing I forgot to tell you."

Clint frowned. Forgotten things often had a habit of being bad news.

"My father," Tessa began, "was a fine man but not very good at business. When he staked his claim, he figured like everyone else that the ore would be just under the surface. He'd been a forty-niner and was used to placer mining. Later on, when they began to understand that the Comstock ore was going to be found deep in the rock, he didn't know how to get down to it. It would take forever to get it out with just a pick and shovel. Up here, you need big mining equipment, dynamite, and timber for shoring up the underground tunnels."

"Sounds expensive," Clint said, studying the dozens of huge mining works and monstrous tailings which dotted the hillsides. It was obvious that all the dirt wasn't brought up in buckets by hand. All over the Comstock you could see steam rising from hoisting works and hear the heavy *thump-thump* of their powerful engines.

"Oh, it was expensive, all right. Most of the miners were men like my father who couldn't even read much less start up a complicated mining company with a payroll and big equipment. So they did what the people from San Francisco and the cities knew they would, they sold out for a few thousand dollars and went away happy."

"And their claims were worth millions."

"Exactly." Tessa frowned. "I was eighteen and living in Sacramento with my aunt and uncle when my father sent for me. My mother had died years ago and father never did stay in one place long enough to give me a home or a place where I could go to school. But I missed him terribly and raced here determined to help him with his new mine any way I could."

Tessa smiled sadly. "The most obvious thing I first noticed was that my father was using a pick and shovel while all the mining companies around him were building hoisting works and pulling the ore out of the ground a hundred times faster. And there was something else, Clint. Their underground tunnels were fanning out in all directions. It didn't take a genius to figure out that big mines like the Golden Eagle were stealing from small claims like my father's."

Clint shook his head. "I understand. And, of course, they'd never let you down into their mines so you'd have any way of proving it."

"Exactly." Tessa sighed. "It was like something eating away your belly, and you couldn't see or even feel it but you knew it was happening. It drove my father crazy. He could see the rich ore coming out of the mines all around him every hour and knew it was his own, and there was nothing he could do to stop it from happening."

"Except sell out like every other poor devil without any backing."

"That's right. But we did have one chance and we took it by borrowing money. We were amazed that a banker would lend us the five thousand we needed to buy a steam engine, cable, a wire hoisting cage, and some other equipment. My father was pathetically grateful even if the interest was seven per cent a month."

Clint whistled. "That's highway robbery!"

"It was a godsend, at least we thought so at the time. It was only later that we came to realize our friendly banker was in King Cleaver's pocket and that the note we signed as collateral was given to King."

"Let me guess the end of this story," Clint said. "The note is all due and payable sometime in the near future and, if you can't pay it off, the Shamrock Mine becomes the property of this King Cleaver and the Sutro Mining Corporation."

"That's right," Tessa said quietly.

"How much time do we have?"

She tried to brighten and give him a brave smile, but she just couldn't. "We have the rest of the summer. Two months."

Clint nodded. He thought about how it was always the little guy who got the short end of the stick. People like Cleaver and the San Francisco bankers were the guys who feasted. On the other side of the table were the poor bastards like O'Grady who'd sweated the deserts and froze in the high mountains, starved and worked like hell all his life to make a strike, only to wind up with crumbs from the big men's tables.

"Do you think we can do it, Clint?"

He slipped his arm around her waist and nodded. "If the mine is operational and we can figure out which direction to start working, I think we can."

"So do I!" Tessa kissed his cheek and hugged him with

gratitude. "I don't know what I'd do without your help. Making you a millionaire is going to be almost as fun as making myself one."

He laughed and said, "Remember Tessa, I don't want your money." Then they mounted, started down from the Divide, and rode out toward the Shamrock Mine. It occurred to Clint that, the moment they crossed onto that property, word would flash to King Cleaver that they had arrived.

It was going to be real interesting to see what would happen after that.

TEN

The Gunsmith studied the pair of strangers who sat guarding the Shamrock Mine. He eased his gun in its holster and frowned because he'd seen enough trouble for one day.

"They wouldn't happen to be friends of yours, would they, Tessa?" he asked hopefully.

"I'm afraid not. What are we going to do?"

"That depends on what they do after I point out that they must be guarding the wrong mine."

Tessa nodded. "I have the deed. We could just find the sheriff and let him take care of them."

Clint had thought of that and rejected the idea. "That would be the easy way but not the best," he said. "King Cleaver probably hired this pair so we might as well let him know we've returned and plan on staying to operate this mine."

They kept riding forward, and when it became obvious to the guards that the two riders were coming to face them, they both threw down their cigarettes and picked up their rifles. "That's about far enough," one warned.

Clint reined Duke to a standstill and said, "Afternoon, boys. Nice day, isn't it?"

They nodded and relaxed a little. "Yeah, it's nice all right, but you've crossed onto private property."

Clint studied the shack that housed the hoisting works. He looked at the platform surrounding the mine shaft. It did not look as though it had been operational for quite some time. It was dark inside the shed, but where rays of sunlight poked through the tin roof, he could see that the steam engine and all the machinery looked rusty and out of commission. Clint did not enjoy machinery of any kind and he wondered how he was going to get this collection of junk running.

He turned his attention back to the guards. He sat loose in the saddle with a smile on his face; he looked like a man who hadn't a care in the world. In fact, the opposite was true. His hand had shifted to within inches of his gun, and though he badly wanted to avoid a shoot-out, he was ready for one.

Tessa was staring at him, a quizzical expression on her face. "Clint, didn't you hear them?"

"I sure did," he said easily. "They said that we had crossed onto private property. I was just wondering exactly where the boundaries of this claim run."

The guards were only too happy to point them out to him— little piles of rock at each of the four corners of the claim.

Clint dismounted and walked to the nearest marker. As in most claims, there was a small tobacco can sitting in the pile with its tin lid pressed down tight against the weather. Clint thumbed the can open, aware that the guards and Tessa had followed him.

Fishing out a piece of paper, Clint unfolded it and read, "This marks the southeast corner of the Shamrock Mine, owned by the Sutro Mining Corporation of Virginia City. Trespassers or thieves will be shot on sight."

He looked at the guards. "There must be some mistake here. This is the Shamrock Mine, but the owner is this young woman, Miss Tessa O'Grady."

Their reaction was predictably slow. Before they could raise their Winchesters, Clint had them covered with his own gun. His draw was so fast he'd caught them completely off guard.

"Drop them!" The way he said it left no doubt that he was not a man who bluffed about such things, and their rifles thud-

THE MINERS' SHOWDOWN

ded to the ground. Tessa scooped them up and moved back.

"I assume you were hired by King Cleaver."

The first man, who was fiftyish and soft-looking and obviously damn worried, shook his head vigorously. "Mace Allard hired us. Mr. Cleaver, he don't mess with such things."

"That's right," the other guard seconded. "And nothing was said about this claim belonging to someone else. We were just supposed to keep people from stealing any machinery or going down the shaft and taking ore. This mountain is overrun with thieves."

"The biggest one being King Cleaver," Tessa said with anger and disgust.

"We're just hired to protect this property, ma'am; neither Jeb nor myself is ready to die for it."

Clint holstered his weapon. These were not dangerous men who had any illusions about their prowess with a gun. "I'm glad to hear that," he said.

"Who the hell are you, mister? I ain't never seen anyone shuck iron the way you just did. And I've had the honor of seeing some of the best."

"Come on, Jeb. That's Clint Adams. He's the Gunsmith!" the other man announced.

Clint scowled. It always made his life a little more complicated knowing that some fool would try to face him and gain a quick reputation. Even worse, now King Cleaver and his henchmen would realize exactly what they were up against.

"Well, I'll be damned! The Gunsmith!" He stuck out his hand. "Sir, it's a real honor. I heard what you did up in the Dakota Territory and in Texas. Your legend stretches from Canada all the way down to South America."

Clint stuck out his hand. When it came to the stories people told about him, he was naturally shy. "The truth is," he said modestly, "people do tend to exaggerate."

"That may be," the guard said, pumping his hand hard. "But Jeb and I saw you shuck that gun and it was nothing but a blur. That wasn't no exaggeration! I've seen Wyatt Earp and Bat Masterson draw, but you'd drill 'em both in their tracks. They'd never even clear leather against your move!"

"I find that hard to believe," Clint said, finally pulling his hand free. "And I'm glad I won't ever have to find out. The thing of it is that right now you and your friend are out of a job."

"We'll find another."

"Maybe you already have."

They stared at him looking puzzled, so Clint elaborated. "Miss O'Grady and I plan to work this mine but we know almost nothing about mining. We could use a couple of good men."

They exchanged nervous glances. "Not me."

"Me either," the second man echoed. "Wouldn't be at all healthy. Not the way things are shaping up."

"We'd protect you," Tessa said quickly.

"You'd try to protect us, but that would be impossible. How are you going to keep watch over this whole mountainside? Why, even if you slept down in the mine, somebody could still sneak up here and throw in a lighted stick of dynamite and blow you to pieces. No thanks, you may be the Gunsmith and I'll never come after you, but there's a hell of a lot of men on Cleaver's payroll who will."

Tessa started to argue, but Clint held up his hand for silence. There was no sense in going any further; these men had no stomach for trouble and would be run off too easily.

"Maybe," Clint said, "you could at least tell us what in the way of machinery we're going to need to get this thing up and running again."

They walked to the shed and pulled the door wide open. One hinge was busted and the other one protested with an angry screeching sound. The machinery inside reminded Clint of nothing more than a pile of rusted junk.

"You got your work cut out for you, Clint. The shaft itself is about fifty feet deep and then there is a cave with tunnels running out in a couple of directions. Without this machinery, though, there's no way you or any high grade ore can get up or down."

"The machinery works!" Tessa said impatiently. "Maybe it just needs oiling."

"Needs a whole lot more than that, ma'am. Before we got here, scavengers were carrying it away piece by piece. They

THE MINERS' SHOWDOWN 49

went in that shed and unbolted everything that they could carry away, and they'd have driven off loaded wagons if we hadn't been sent to keep them away. Guess you do owe Mr. Cleaver and Sutro for that."

"I'll thank the man first chance," Clint said with more than a hint of sarcasm. "What do we need?"

The man walked inside the weathered old shack and spent five minutes in frowning silence. Finally, he pulled a pencil out of his pocket and began to scribble some list on a scrap of paper. "Best I write it out so you'll remember."

"I appreciate that. I also need to have some idea of the costs," Clint said.

"Cost is going to be around a thousand dollars."

"A thousand dollars!" Tessa cried. "We don't have that kind of money, do we, Clint?"

The way she asked, then looked so hopefully up at him made Clint shift uneasily. "Tessa, you know I'm not a wealthy man. I've got about two, maybe three hundred dollars and that's all."

"Well, that's all right. It's a start at least and..."

"Whoa! I've never said anything about spending all my money on this mine. That wasn't part of the deal."

"Awww, c'mon Clint. What's a few hundred dollars in a place like this? We are standing on a claim worth millions!" She kissed his cheek and her finger played provocatively with the top button of his shirt.

"Now," she purred, "you aren't going to have me throw away millions for want of pocket change, are you?"

He almost had to laugh. Maybe Tessa hadn't had a lot of men, but she sure did understand how to get what she wanted out of them.

Besides, he was a gambler, always had been, and always would be. Clint began to hedge a little. "I just never allow myself or Duke to be flat broke. He and I both enjoy eating too much."

Tessa smiled. "Then we'll keep a few dollars for food and hay. I just don't understand why a couple of pieces of metal cost so much."

The guard handed Clint the scrap of paper. "You give that

to most any of the machinery dealers up here and they'll know what it is you need. If you're lucky, they'll be able to get it in California or even from some mine nearby that's either folded or has replaced its machinery with bigger stuff. That way, you could be working in just a week or so. Otherwise, they'll have to send your order back east and then ship the parts around the Horn of South America. Could easily take months."

"We don't have months," Clint said, thinking about that five-thousand-dollar note that was due in just under sixty days.

"Yeah, so I gather. And the machinery people won't take an order without cash. I'd say that's your first problem."

The other guard, a smallish fellow with thin red hair and chapped lips, scrubbed his whiskers. "That's one of the best horses I ever saw anywhere. He'd fetch a thousand easy."

Clint's reaction was swift and blunt. "The hell with that. If I were dying of hunger, I'd still not part with Duke for food or money. We'll figure out something else." He folded the list of missing parts they'd need and put the paper into his vest pocket. "Thanks for your help."

"Suppose we could have those rifles back?"

"Do they belong to you or the Sutro Mining Corporation?"

"The Sutro."

"Then they stay. You tell your boss I'd like to meet him out here. Tell him I'll be waiting with those rifles if he has the courage to come get them."

The guard nodded. "He won't come. But there will be others who will, Gunsmith."

"Let them. Just don't be with them."

"Bet on it! Good luck to the both of you."

Both Clint and Tessa watched them walk away. Tessa said, "They're nice men. I think they'd have liked to help us."

"They would have," Clint said. "But I've got a real bad feeling that—for us at least—help is going to be damned hard to come by."

ELEVEN

Virginia City was awash in money. Every saloon and cafe was filled to overflowing with miners from around the world. In less than one city block you could hear the coarse language of the great miners from Wales and then catch the strident, nasal laughter of the Irishmen. But there were also English, French, Spanish, Mexican, African, and even Australian fortune seekers. And every one of them seemed to be spending money like there was no tomorrow.

The Chinese were the least rowdy nationality. They had their own sector of the city where they seemed to flourish with their laundries, opium dens, joss houses, and markets. They were a hardy and generally industrious people many of whom had come over at the expense of the Central Pacific Railroad Company to lay the transcontinental track from Sacramento to Promontory Point in the Utah Territory. They were sharp traders, people who loved to haggle over prices.

There were clusters of Indians, too. Paiutes mostly, men and women who stayed together and seemed dazed by all the frenzied activity. This had once been their mountain, their land.

Seeing them begging for handouts or even asking for menial jobs gave the Gunsmith an uneasy feeling. The Paiutes had raided the Pony Express and attacked early wagon trains filled with immigrants, but not until their precious pines had been stripped, their deer and game depleted, and their water sources fouled by a tidal wave of California-bound forty-niners.

Tessa attracted the attention of every man on C Street. She turned the heads of entire crowds and brought appreciative stares and whistles when they passed. Tessa seemed to enjoy their attention. It wasn't rare to see a beautiful young woman on these rough boardwalks, but it was unusual to see one who wasn't hustling business for herself and her friends over in the thriving red light district. Fortunately, not one of the hundreds of men they passed was crude or obnoxious. Tessa was a looker, but there was also something about her that commanded respect and let men know she was not nor ever would be a whore.

"Well," she said, as they stood before a large and impressive bank on B Street. "This is the biggest one on the Comstock. I guess we might as well get our money right here and now."

The bank was a two-story affair with big windows. The place was filled with men—not the rough, drunken kinds he'd seen out on the streets, but prosperous types mostly, and respectable women he took to be the wives of merchants and mine operators.

Clint had changed into a clean set of clothes and even wore a fine broadcloth jacket, but he stopped short of wearing round-toed city shoes or a constricting tie. The only important distinction between himself and the other men inside was that he wore his gun just as naturally as if it were a part of his body. The gun and the confident way he moved gave people the idea he was probably a famous lawman, perhaps a Pinkerton detective or Wells Fargo agent on some important case; but the stylish cut of his coat and his own raffish good looks also gave the impression that Clint was a highly successful, professional gambler or wealthy patron of the theater.

Except for the part about being wealthy, the Gunsmith was all of those things and a whole lot more. As Tessa linked her arm through his and gazed at their reflection in the window, she thought Clint was about the handsomest man she'd ever laid eyes on. Her chest swelled with pride, and she blushed from the sudden warmth she felt rising from between her legs. She had absolute confidence that they'd be successful in getting the thousand dollars they'd need to get the Shamrock Mine operating again; in fact, she'd decided to ask for the additional five thousand so that she could pay off the note due in less than sixty days. Not that they'd need to—they'd probably strike it rich long before then, but it never hurt to play it safe.

Clint surveyed the long lines leading up to the four tellers. Clint hated lines, refused to join them unless there was absolutely no choice in the matter. He studied the small offices beyond the wooden divider.

"There," he said, pointing toward the largest private office and the dignified old gentleman who sat scowling and looking over papers on his desk. "Unless I miss my guess, that is the bank president and I've never seen any sense in starting at the bottom of the ladder in these things. We'll pay him a visit."

"But Clint, we can't just barge in there! It says on that sign that..."

Clint did not care what the sign said. The man was a banker and they were prospective clients willing to pay a reasonable interest on a loan.

"Sir!"

At least three junior bank executives jumped from their desks and rushed at Clint, but he ignored them. One young, bespectacled teller managed to get between him and the bank president's doorway, but when he looked into the Gunsmith's eyes he wilted like a blade of chopped meadow grass.

"Good afternoon!" Clint hailed from the doorway.

"My name is Clint Adams and this is Miss Tessa O'Grady. We come to talk to you about a loan."

"Please, sir!" a frantic bank executive cried, tugging at Clint's sleeve. "You can't do this. Only..."

The old man at the desk looked up and bellowed, "Well, he obviously has already done it, Stilpepper! Who let him in here in the first place!"

Tessa pushed between them. "No one did, sir. We are uninvited but... but you have such a wonderful reputation for good will, honesty, and helping people that we just could not wait to meet someone so prominent as yourself!"

As Clint watched in amazement, Tessa rushed forward and grabbed the old bank president's hand and wrung it like a wet rag. "What an honor this is! Everyone speaks so highly of you, Mister..."—she glanced down at his deskplate—"Mr. Bainsworthy!"

"Who said all those things about me?" he asked skeptically.

Tessa did not even blink. "Everyone who's ever had the honor of doing business with you, sir. Everyone in this city who counts for anything."

His resistance crumbled like a month-old cookie. "Well, now! I have provided some small service to the leading citizens of Virginia City."

"Of course, you have. That's why we wouldn't have dreamed of going to any other than the Bank of..."

"Virginia City," Clint finished.

Tessa drew up a seat across from him while Clint just shook his head in simple admiration. Amazing.

"Yes, the Bank of Virginia City. A pillar of professionalism. A tribute to your foresight and dedication, your wisdom and..."

"Oh, come, come now!" The banker leaned forward eagerly. Clint noticed he could not confine his glance to Tessa's face. "Enough of your wonderful words of appreciation. How much do you need and for what purpose?"

"Six thousand dollars. Enough to pay off a terrible note at the rate of seven per cent per month and..."

"Seven per cent! That's outrageous!"

"Our feeling exactly," Tessa said. "I'm so glad you agree. Anyway, we need to pay it off before it comes due and to buy parts to repair our mining equipment."

"That seems very reasonable," he said, hurriedly polishing his spectacles, then shoving them back in place, and leaning farther forward until his face was within a foot of the swell of Tessa's wonderful breasts. "Very reasonable."

"Oh, thank you, Mr. Bainsworthy! Can we have the money right now?"

The man behind Clint coughed loud and long. It seemed to pull the bank president out of his momentary daze when he added, "We'll need security, sir."

THE MINERS' SHOWDOWN

Clint wanted to pound a sharp elbow into his belly but the damage was already done.

"Oh, yes. I... I'm afraid we must have something as security for the loan, Miss O'Grady. It's the bank policy and even I cannot ignore the rules—especially since I made them."

Tessa knew the spell was broken, the game perhaps lost. But to her credit, she just smiled and produced the deed. "As you can see by the location, this mining claim is as good as gold."

Bainsworthy stared at the deed for a long, long time before he looked up, and when he did his eyes had lost their sparkle. He swallowed and said in a very subdued voice, "I'm afraid this bank cannot help you, my dear woman. You'll have to excuse me now."

"What do you mean," Tessa whispered, "just a..."

Clint stepped forward. "He means he is owned by King Cleaver and Sutro Mining and that he doesn't dare help us."

The man's head snapped up. He opened his mouth to speak but no words came out, and finally he looked back down and began to shuffle his papers listlessly. Clint took Tessa by the arm and helped her to her feet. At the doorway to the private office, the young executive, who had a more than coincidental resemblance to his father, sneered. "Bank rules," he said smugly.

Clint stomped his heel down hard on the man's toes, saw the smile change into a look of twisted agony and the blood drain from his face. Then he and Tessa O'Grady marched out of the bank.

Once outside, Tessa leaned up against him. "What do we do now?" she sighed. "If the biggest banker on the Comstock is under King Cleaver's thumb, I don't think we'll have much chance getting a loan anywhere else."

There was more than a small measure of truth to what she said, Clint thought grimly. He took a deep breath. "There's more than one way to skin a cat," he said. "And there are a couple thousand men here with a lot of money. I'll figure out something, so don't you worry about it any longer."

"I just don't want you to have to do anything dangerous, Clint. I'd rather lose the mine than see you killed."

He kissed her for saying that. "I know you would, Tessa.

And that's why I'm going to all this bother."

Clint took her arm then and started walking. He decided that it would be a waste of time to go to any other bank. As soon as they looked at the deed and realized it was adjoining the Golden Eagle owned by Sutro Mining, they'd be turned down again.

Maybe, Clint thought grimly, it was time to pay a visit to King Cleaver and his friends. Sometimes, the best way to go at a problem was to lower your head and go right straight at it full tilt. Yep, he thought, it was time to take the bull by the horns.

TWELVE

The Gunsmith took Tessa back to their claim and it seemed only natural that he asked her to remain there on guard against thieves until he returned.

"What are you going to do?" she asked.

"I have a friend or two who might be able to lend us the money."

Tessa's eyes brightened with hope. "You tell them I agree to pay a good rate of interest."

The Gunsmith smiled. "My friends don't charge interest. But they'll appreciate the offer."

And though it was less than a mile back up to the city, Clint rode Duke. There were any number of stables in Virginia City and he'd decided to find the best one and board the big black gelding until he was ready to leave. He had a feeling that there was going to be trouble and he didn't want Duke to get caught in the line of fire when the bullets started flying.

When he located the best stable and left the gelding in the comfort of a straw-filled barn, Clint obtained directions to the Sutro Mining Corporation's headquarters and started off on foot.

He was well aware that the man he'd winged at Lake Tahoe and who had escaped might be there and recognize him the moment he walked into those offices. If that happened, there might be a battle right away and he'd have to shoot his way in to see King Cleaver. But he figured that the last thing these people would want would be an open gunfight. They just didn't need to take that sort of risk. No, he decided, King Cleaver would see him, probably even be cordial enough to give him a fair warning to leave the Comstock before he set his dogs loose.

Clint reached the impressive offices of Sutro and pulled his hat down tight. He figured maybe he ought to be the one who did the warning.

"Can I help you?" a young man inquired.

Clint eyed the man who looked at him with more than casual interest. At first glance, he appeared to be some kind of clerk; only then did he notice that he wore a tied-down gun on his hip, and he realized he was a hired gunman.

"I'd like to see your boss."

"Mr. Allard? I'm afraid he's out."

"Not him," Clint said eyeing a solid mahogany door. "I want to see Mr. Cleaver."

The man's congenial smile faded. "And who the hell are you?"

"Clint Adams. What's your name?"

The young gunman stiffened. Clint was reminded of the way a dog's hair began to rise on its back just before a fight.

"My name is Cole Sheppard. I've been looking forward to meeting you, Gunsmith."

Clint frowned. "I want to see Cleaver, not get into a gunfight."

"You might not have any choice," the man said, starting to ease his hand down toward his gun.

Clint did the only thing that made sense at the moment. He smashed the young gunfighter a wicked blow to his chin and drove him over backward. Then, the man slid down the wall and rolled over onto the floor. He bent down and removed his gun, emptied the cartridges and stuffed them into his pocket before replacing the empty weapon back into its holster.

THE MINERS' SHOWDOWN

He rubbed his stinging knuckles and frowned, wondering how many more times he was going to have to face some younger man who was foolish enough to think the risk of dying was worth being known as the man who outdrew and killed the Gunsmith. Seven years ago he might have drawn his gun and killed this man in self-defense. But he was growing tired of killing, and even now he still clung to the faint hope that perhaps King Cleaver would give up this game and allow Tessa to work the Shamrock Mine in peace. After all, how much money did one man need in this world?

Clint did not bother to knock but walked right into what instantly shaped up as some kind of meeting. There were five men, all business types and prosperous looking. But it was King Cleaver who gripped immediate attention. He dominated the room so completely that everyone else seemed to fade into the woodwork.

King Cleaver was a man of immense proportions. He was fat and had to weigh at least three hundred pounds. His face was as round as a ball and shaven just like the top of his head so that his features were a smooth series of rolls that glistened with oily sweat. His eyes were like little raisins shoved into dough and his mouth seemed much too small to accept the enormous amount of food that it would take to feed that great, bloated body. When he spoke, his lips seemed to move as if they were disconnected from his face. His voice was high, almost womanish.

"Who are you and what is the meaning of this intrusion?" he hissed. "Cole, Cole throw this..."

"I'm afraid Cole is temporarily out of commission. He's taking a short siesta."

Cleaver's eyes flicked to the open doorway, then back to Clint. "I see," he said, "and what can I do for you, Gunsmith?"

"Well, news travels fast. I wasn't sure that you'd heard I was in town. I guess you are probably also aware that I'm helping Tessa O'Grady work her mine."

King smiled and it was obscene. "Ah, yes! Dear lovely little Tessa. Fine young woman—the kind who could easily turn any man's head, make him do something foolish and even very dangerous."

"Yes, I suppose."

King nodded. "I would think that she'd give a man a good . . ."

The words died in his throat when he saw the Gunsmith's expression change. "Well, never mind," he added quickly. "I am obviously disappointed in the both of you, for you should know how much I want that claim."

"I saw your men trying to kill Tessa up at Lake Tahoe. That pretty well says it all."

"You've no proof that they were my men."

"There might come a day when, proof or no proof, I'll put a bullet through you."

"I'm not worried about it," he said. "I know all about you, Mr. Adams. You were a lawman too long to murder me or anyone else. The only way you'd kill me would be in self-defense and I assure you I will never try to take your life."

Clint sneered. "Of course, you won't. You'll have your hired men take all the risks. You don't have the guts to face a man on your own."

Cleaver chuckled. "You can't insult me, Adams. A man of your stature is nothing. You are way out of your league. Be smart. Convince the girl to sell the claim. I'll give her a fair price."

"How much?"

He pursed his lips and Clint was reminded of a fish. "I'll offer her . . . oh, let's be generous and say forty thousand dollars. That's twenty thousand you can put in your own pocket and ride away with, if you want to cut yourself in. Take the girl with you! Use her until she gets tiresome, then leave her. It's a very attractive offer when you think it out."

"Not when you stack forty thousand up against a few million we believe the mine is worth."

King barked with coarse laughter. "A few million! You are as big a dreamer as old man O'Grady used to be!"

"Where is he buried?"

"How should I know?"

Clint walked up and leaned forward on the massive desk. Up close, King was even more repulsive than he was from across the room. He was wearing some kind of French cologne

THE MINERS' SHOWDOWN

and it stank. "Make even one wrong move against me and I'm coming after you."

Cleaver reared back and his body began to quiver like a bowstring. "You don't scare me," he hissed. "You've just made a terrible error in judgment. These men are now witnesses that you have threatened to kill me. If you do, I guarantee that you'll hang and that Tessa O'Grady will live only long enough to curse the day she met you."

Clint ached to reach across the desk and grab this man and choke the poisoned life out of him. But he would hang for that and King wasn't worth anyone dying.

"You've been warned."

"Freeze, Gunsmith!"

Clint spun around to see Cole Sheppard, nose still dripping blood, with his gun pointed right at Clint and ready to fire. The young man's face was contorted with hatred and the gun was shaking violently.

"You can't get a reputation by shooting me down without a fair chance to draw on you," Clint said.

Sheppard's eyes darted to those of King Cleaver and the man nodded with approval. Sheppard took a deep breath and holstered his gun. His hands dropped to his side and his fingers twitched eagerly. "You're ripe, past your prime, Gunsmith."

"We'll see. Go ahead and draw—if you've the stomach."

Sheppard swallowed nervously. He was scared to death but pride overran fear and Clint waited while he screwed his courage up and made his play.

"You are mighty young to die—especially for the sake of a reptile like King Cleaver."

"Take him Cole! Do it now!" King shrieked.

Sheppard blinked, then made his play. He was very fast but reckless, and his hand struck his gun a little off center. It didn't matter. Clint could have outdrawn him anyway but he drew and watched the man shrink in terror.

"Oh, Jesus! Don't kill me!" the young gunman begged.

Clint gave the situation a good long bit of consideration and finally holstered his gun in disgust. He turned to Cleaver and said, "Good men are damned hard to find, aren't they?"

Then he walked out of the room.

"Gunsmith!"

He froze.

"Turn around goddamn you!"

Clint sighed and did as he was ordered, knowing what was going to happen next. He faced the younger man who was half-crazed with hatred and humiliation. "You shamed me!"

"You shamed yourself." Clint forced a smile. "Do yourself a big favor and put the gun away before I'm obliged to kill you."

Sheppard blinked with amazement. Then he began to giggle. "You hear that, Mr. Cleaver? He thinks he can draw and shoot me before I can even pull the trigger! The famous Gunsmith must believe everything that's been said and written about him!"

"Put the gun away, Cole," Clint said.

The man shook his head violently. "Not after what you did to me. Not after that! Draw Gunsmith!"

There was no choice. His hand went for his gun, but this time with reluctance. Cole Sheppard waited until he started to lift his gun and then he pulled his own trigger.

The gun clicked on an empty cylinder. Terror flooded into his eyes and he began to pull the trigger. That's when Clint walked up to him and decked him.

From the strength of his blow and the grimace on Cole's face as the fist destroyed his jaw, they all knew Cole had learned his lesson and would never take on the Gunsmith again.

Four of the five men were so astonished they nodded in agreement. And the fifth, well, words couldn't describe the venomous look of shock on King Cleaver's face and the way his little lips sputtered with spit and fury.

Clint walked out of the offices of the Sutro Mining Corporation feeling no joy or satisfaction.

He'd given Cole Sheppard every chance but the man had proven himself to be cowardly and he had deserved what he got. But that didn't help anything and it sure didn't help him find the money he and Tessa so badly needed.

Clint reached into his pocket and pulled out his wallet and slowly counted his money. Two hundred even. He glanced up and down the street, then started for the nearest saloon where he'd find a poker table. There was more than one way to skin a cat and he just hoped his luck might start turning. If not, they were in big trouble, he and Tessa.

Big trouble, indeed.

THIRTEEN

The hour was approaching midnight and the Gunsmith had made only a hundred dollars after six hours of concentrated poker playing. He was not a professional gambler, but he was good enough to win usually. The problem was that Virginia City had attracted every professional west of the Mississippi River. There wasn't a single table on the entire Comstock that didn't have at least one of them sitting in on a game.

That was discouraging because that meant the games were rigged in some way. Clint knew that it wasn't easy to spot a professional cheater—those who were inept never lasted very long. If discovered, they'd be shot or run out of town and warned not to return. Since there was such a fortune to be made on the Comstock, the cheaters were especially clever. There were a lot of ways to tilt the odds in a gambler's favor and Clint thought he knew most of them. Some gamblers specialized in shaving the card's edges with a razor so that a very delicate touch could detect and read the card's value; those cards were called strippers. Other gamblers mastered holding out cards so well that it was almost impossible to catch them drawing that extra ace.

THE MINERS' SHOWDOWN

One of the most difficult things to detect was a well-marked deck. Marking cards was an art and some gamblers took as much pride in marking the cards as they did in using them during a game. They considered themselves artists in filling in or altering the filligree usually found on the backs of cards.

Clint had joined in no less than four different games in four different saloons and gambling halls in search of an honest game before he decided that it was going to be impossible. That left him no choice but to try to learn the cheater's system in order to win some real money.

He entered a big saloon called the Bucket of Blood, walked up to the bar, and ordered his whiskey. When it came, he barely even sipped it as he listened to the loud talk of gold and silver, stock prices, and new strikes being made down in Six-Mile Canyon. The crowd was boisterous and hard-drinking. The miners he saw were from many lands, but they all had a sort of sallow look that came from being too long underground and breathing foul, hot air. Clint learned that the Comstock was riddled with hot caverns filled with scalding water and that many a poor miner had buried his pick or drill through a thin wall of rock and been instantly boiled to death.

Clint tried not to think of such things. He promised himself that he would take no chances and allow himself plenty of time above ground so that he'd not become pale and yellow-faced like so many of these young men.

He watched the poker games because he favored them over faro or monte. The Bucket of Blood had six poker games in progress, and he picked up his drink and strolled through the crowd watching each of them for a minute or two before moving on. There was a rule that, if a person wasn't sitting in on the game, he stayed away so that there was no question about spying for one of the active players. It was a good rule, but teams of cheaters still managed to pass behind a cardplayer at just the right moment and then deftly signal out his hand.

Clint had no intention of cheating though he did know how to use a deck skillfully enough to give the impression the cards were being shuffled when they actually were not. He could also deal from the bottom of the deck so well that he could fool most professionals—his theory was that a person had to be able to cheat in order to catch a cheater.

He chose a game that seemed to have only one professional gambler instead of two, which was often the case. If two cheaters were playing against the table, they were almost impossible to catch because, as soon as the victims began to get suspicious of one gambler, he'd start playing honest while his partner began to clean the table. They'd split later and no one would ever be the wiser.

"Mind if I join in?" he asked, motioning toward an empty seat.

The miners had no objections and the professional, who looked at him with unconcealed dislike, had no choice but to nod agreeably. The professional was young, thin, and nervous; Clint was hoping his lack of experience would show under pressure. Clint had every intention of letting the gambler win steadily until there came a crucial hand with heavy betting. Then he'd expose the cheater and pocket his winnings and clear out for the Shamrock Mine. With luck he could easily win over a thousand dollars on the single turn of a card. He'd only have one chance, though, because after that he'd be a marked man himself, one of the professionals, and he'd never have another such opportunity again.

"Hey, aren't you the Gunsmith?" the gambler asked.

"I've been called that in the past," Clint answered reluctantly. Trying to change the subject, he added, "What are we playing?"

"Five card draw," the miners told him. The gambler said nothing because he knew the Gunsmith was purposefully playing it dumb.

"My favorite," Clint said pitching in a five dollar ante. He leaned back in his chair and let the gambler deal him his cards. As expected, they were terrible and he lost five more dollars on that hand and the next few hands were no better.

Clint wasn't interested in winning—not just yet anyway. He wanted to figure the gambler's edge first and the only way he could do that was to lose steadily and without complaint for a good long while until the big hand finally came and the opportunity was ripe for a killing. When that moment came, Clint knew that few men could resist taking chances.

THE MINERS' SHOWDOWN

By two in the morning he was down to eighty dollars and still hadn't quite figured out the gambler's edge. The man did not deal off the bottom of the deck, his shuffle wasn't rigged, and he sure didn't seem to be pulling cards out from his sleeve. As far as Clint could tell, there was no accomplice circling the game and passing signals, and the cards weren't marked.

And yet, Clint knew the man was cheating because he was just too damn lucky. The poker chips were piled high before him and he'd fleeced a string of hard drinking miners. All in all, Clint studied that pile and guessed the man had at least fifteen hundred dollars in winnings. It was time to end the game, yet he still had to figure the edge or he was going to get cleaned out.

"Jesus Christ!" a big miner shouted throwing down his cards in disgust. "I have three kings and you have a damn full house. I'm busted."

The gambler was trained well and very smart, and it showed because he pitched twenty dollars at the big miner and said, "Here, I never like to have a man walk away busted and feeling bad. Your luck will change next time and I'll be here when it does."

The miner stared at the chips with amazement. He wasn't used to such generosity and the sour look on his face was replaced by one of genuine gratitude. "Well, that is damn decent of you, mister! Damn decent!"

He reached out and clasped the gambler's hand in his big, work-roughened paw and shook it heartily.

The gambler's face drained, registering the pain he felt, and Clint leaned forward with sudden intensity. His eyes dropped to the gambler's hand and then he knew the man's edge. He'd used sandpaper on his palms and the tips of his fingers until they had almost bled but were sensitive enough for him to read minute thumbnail indentations. That was why he reacted with so much pain and why he was winning.

Clint said nothing. He took the deal and let his own fingers brush lightly across the backs of his cards, trying to figure out just how they'd been marked. When he thought he felt the faint thumbnail indentation, he tried other cards until he finally had the gambler's secret code figured out.

Thirty minutes later, he had his chance. Even though his own hand was nothing, and even though he had to throw in a gold watch easily worth four hundred dollars because of its fine European workmanship, he stayed in the game.

"It's just you and me," Clint said. "How'd you like to go double or nothing?"

The young gambler smiled and shook his head. "Fine, Mister, but you haven't anything left to bet."

Clint smiled back. He looked around the table at the watchful spectators. He reached down and unbuckled his gunbelt and laid it down on the poker table before him. "I've been offered as much as five thousand dollars for this gun and you can sell it right here and now for at least two thousand."

Clint smiled. He stared the gambler right in the eye and said, "Your pile against my gun. Have we got a bet?"

The gambler swallowed nervously. He had read the cards Clint now held and he knew the Gunsmith had to be bluffing.

"I think you're bluffing," he said with a tight, nervous smile as he pushed his stack of chips into the center of the table. "And I'll..."

"I'll raise you fifty cents," Clint said quickly.

"What!"

The crowd began to hum with excited speculation.

Why would the Gunsmith bet his famous gun and then, when the raise was met, quickly raise the bet by just fifty cents? It didn't make any sense at all!

"Fifty cents more is going to be the price you pay to see what kind of hand I've got." Clint's eyes narrowed, "Fifty cents more or your life if you've been cheating me and these other men."

The gambler stood up quickly. He was armed and no professional man in his trade could afford to be called a cheater— not if he expected to stay in business in Comstock.

Clint smiled coldly. "I didn't say you were cheating; I said 'if you've been cheating.' Big difference. If I'm wrong, maybe we can shake hands."

The gambler stared at him.

"But then," Clint added, "I can tell that you are not a man who enjoys shaking hands very much. I guess those fingers

THE MINERS' SHOWDOWN 69

and hands of yours are the tools of your trade. Just like this gun is mine. Do you want to shake my hand, friend?"

The gambler took a step back; Clint's unspoken meaning was deadly clear. "I don't believe I do," he choked. "I no longer think you are bluffing. And that's all the money I have in the world."

"Well, fer Chrissake!" a spectator growled. "I'll pay the fifty cents rather than see you fold and never know if the Gunsmith really was bluffing."

Clint said, "Stay out of this. This bet is between him and me." He looked deep into the young cardsharp's frightened eyes. "If you don't want to shake my hand and you don't want to match my fifty cent raise, then you're going to have to fold, aren't you?"

"Yeah. Yeah, I am!" the gambler said eagerly. "That's exactly what I aim to do, Gunsmith. I fold." He was almost laughing with relief.

Clint relaxed. He reached down and grabbed his holster and gun and strapped them on. Then he took the gambler's pile of chips, all except for one worth twenty dollars. "You learn fast," he said, "maybe some other day."

The young gambler shook his head. "I don't think I'll ever want another lesson from you. You're too damned expensive."

"Just be thankful the price wasn't much higher," Clint said quietly.

"Believe me, I am," the gambler sighed. And then he hurried away.

Clint bought the house two rounds of drinks and it was nearly two o'clock in the morning before he got ready to leave because everyone on the Comstock seemed to want to buy him drinks.

All in all, things had worked out pretty well. He had enough money to buy the necessary replacement parts and a little left over for expenses. Tessa would be worried, but when he showed her the money she'd be grateful. And a grateful Tessa was well worth any man's trouble.

Clint pocketed the money and headed for the door. He thought of how Tessa would feel in his arms tonight and especially how those luscious breasts of hers would taste.

Clint reeled as a huge ball of fire seemed to erupt behind his eyes. He tried to fight and call for help but he fell into an alley and hit the ground, rolling downhill. He could hear two men cursing and running after him.

Clint figured things were going to get a whole lot worse before they got any better.

FOURTEEN

They didn't want to shoot him because there were just too many people around. No, Clint thought as he rolled faster and faster down the narrow alley, they will try to beat me to death and maybe then they'll pitch me down some deserted mine shaft so that people will say it was an accident.

Clint tried to stop rolling but the blow to his head had left him half-paralyzed and he had no strength. When he began to slow down, he clawed for a handhold but the rocky hillside tore into his palms and he could get none. But they were coming, and when he looked up he could see they both had pipes and if they hadn't been falling and sliding themselves, they'd have finished him by now.

He reached for his gun and forced himself to make his fingers wind themselves securely around that gun before he made his draw. He was seeing double and the light was bad, yet the first man he aimed at was so close that it would have been almost impossible to miss. Clint's gun erupted with a flame and his bullet caught the man and spun him off balance. He cried and went down in a pile and Clint fired a second shot that brought a cry from his partner, who dived into the shadows, then reversed his direction, and took off running back up toward C Street.

Clint returned his attention to the man he'd shot. His own head was swimming and he still could not focus. He managed to crawl to the man and grab his wrist. There was no pulse.

"Help!" Clint cried hoarsely. "I need some help down here!"

He reached back and felt blood soaking into his hair. That first blow had been a vicious one and he hoped it had been the dead man at his side who'd delivered it. Clint tried to rise to his hands and knees, but there was just no strength at all left in him. He needed to rest a few minutes. The world was spinning much too fast and he felt that he had to hang onto it tightly or he'd be thrown off.

Clint laid his bloodied head on his forearm, pistol still in his hand. He would rest a few minutes and then he'd get back to the safety of the Shamrock Mine. Back to the warmth of Tessa. Yes, he thought dizzily as his fingers dug into the hard, rocky mountainside.

All I need is just a few minutes to rest. And then I'll feel better.

When he awoke, it was like heaven. He could feel Tessa underneath the blankets. Clint signed happily. He was glad Tessa wasn't angry because he'd been gone so long and he was glad that some kind soul had found him and brought him to her. Later, he'd tell her all about what had happened, but not now.

He stared into the darkness and concentrated on what she was doing to his body. When her tongue darted out to lick the head of his cock, he closed his eyes and groaned with pleasure as the warm, wet cavern of her mouth took him and began to suck.

"Oh, yeah," he breathed. "You are doing fine. You're the best ever. Don't stop."

She appreciated the compliment and sucked him even harder and her soft hands gently massaged his balls until they ached with a pleasure that was almost painful but which he wanted never to end. He began to rotate his hips and her fingernails

THE MINERS' SHOWDOWN

dug with fierce determination into his buttocks and he liked that just fine, too. Clint forgot about his own pain; the ache in his head was overridden now by the ache in his balls and by his desire.

"Now it's my turn," he breathed. Climbing up, he entered her. He began to rotate his hips and she reached around to hold his buttocks, keeping him in her as deep as she could every single moment. He began to piston in and out, slow and deep at first, then faster and faster until he was slamming into her and she was grunting and moaning and pounding him.

"Do me! Do me, Clint! Now!"

When she whispered this into his ear, he just went crazy and his body began to unleash all the fury and seed it held. She threw her head back and wailed like a she-cat in a dark alley.

It took him a full two minutes before he wanted to stop pumping her and she stopped milking him for every drop he had left. It took several more minutes before he caught his breath and said, "I have to say this, Tessa, you're a match for any woman I ever had."

She gently kissed his cheek. "Clint, darlin', I don't quite know how to tell you this, but I'm not Tessa; this is your Honey Bare!"

He pushed himself up and off her and stared down, but it was pitch dark. She felt like Tessa. But then he remembered Honey Bare down in El Paso, Texas and she also felt like Tessa, or vice versa. "This is Honey Bare?"

"If you don't know it by now," she said a little peevishly, "you never will."

He chuckled. "I believe you. Don't know how I got here but you sure have a fine way of bringing a man back to life."

She gave him a little kiss and hug. "Clint, darlin', I been thinking about you ever since we spent that time together in Honey Bare's Hideaway."

"You had seven girls then; how many are you working now?"

"Almost twenty," she said proudly. "I'm the biggest, the richest, the sexiest madame on the Comstock and you are the only man I'm wanting."

Clint laughed. Honey Bare had never been one to play

games. If she hated someone, she said so, but if she really liked... there wasn't anything in the world she wouldn't do. The time he'd spent with her in El Paso had been special and, if it weren't for Tessa O'Grady and her Shamrock Mine, he'd have been more than happy to take up where they left off.

"I can't stay," he said quietly. "There's a young woman and I have to help her work her claim."

"Miners come cheap. I'll hire a couple to take your place."

"Uh-uh," he grunted. "It gets a whole lot more complicated than that."

Honey Bare was silent for a long moment. Then she reached down and began to massage his limp cock. "Sounds bad for me, Clint. I've got it in my mind to change yours. Want to bet that I can't?"

He kissed her mouth, then sighed with pleasure as she began to make him hard again. "Honey Bare," he said with a laugh, "in your bed, a man would be a fool to bet against you."

She began to slide back down on him. "Clint, darlin', I'm going to make you forget you ever heard of that Tessa O'Grady. At least for tonight I am!"

Clint closed his eyes. He wasn't about to argue with her.

FIFTEEN

When Clint awoke the next morning, Honey Bare was still sleeping. He arose, moved to a chair that had his clothes draped over it, and quietly dressed. Pushing the window curtains open, he looked down into the street below and noted that it was already filled with ore and supply wagons. A stagecoach thundered by scattering a couple of drunken miners, who picked themselves out of the dust and shouted obscenities in a foreign language.

Two doors away, piano music rolled out into the crowded street, and he could hear loud guffaws and laughter. That was the way it was in Virginia City. With the big mines carrying up to one hundred men and working twenty-four hours a day, the action never stopped. Miners climbing out of the earth at six o'clock in the morning were ready to have a few drinks and raise some hell. The bartenders never stopped pouring drinks and the prostitutes never stopped working.

Clint had a panoramic view to the east; he could see the barren mountains of Nevada unfolding into a hazy infinity. A little to the north he saw the cemetery and it was three times as big as it had been the last time he'd visited this town. Men and women died young in Virginia City. It was a hard area, freezing in the winter and hot in the summer. Miners died almost nightly in the saloons over cards or curses. There were muggers and murderers lurking in the alleys and Clint knew he should have been more careful last night. But they hadn't gotten his winnings. Come to think of it, they hadn't seemed interested in robbing him—they'd tried to beat him to death.

Clint frowned. If that were true, the only explanation possible for that vicious attack was that it was premeditated—that they'd been waiting just for him. And it didn't take a whole lot of brainpower to figure out why. King Cleaver and the Sutro Mining Corporation had sent them to kill him—make it all look like just another mugging where the victim happened to have had his skull crushed.

There was a terrible knot the size of a hen's egg on the back of his head and his hair was matted with dried blood. Clint's mouth drew into a tight, hard line. He was going to have to be more careful.

"Clint?"

He turned around. "Morning, Honey." He studied her and thought that, if anything, she was even better looking than she'd been down in El Paso. Apparently, the thin, brisk air of the Comstock and the steady stream of gold into her thriving business had combined to make her flourish.

"Come here on the bed and sit down with me. But first, will you open the door and yell out for some coffee."

He did as she asked, though he felt a little silly yelling out into an empty hallway. When he closed the door, he said, "This is a hell of a nice place you have here. Oriental rugs, antique furniture, and good art. Honey, you really must be doing a good business."

"I'm getting rich, Clint. This is the best I've ever seen. Bigger and better than anything I ever did in the California gold fields. Even better than it was for me in San Francisco."

Clint remembered that Honey Bare had become the most famous prostitute in California ten years earlier. She'd had men standing in line to pay her five hundred dollars for a single night and she'd been damned choosy about whom she'd picked.

THE MINERS' SHOWDOWN

Later, when she'd opened her first whorehouse in San Francisco, she'd been an immediate success and had prospered enough to build a clientele that included only the most prominent and successful men in that city. Clint had never understood why she'd moved to El Paso. He had heard rumors that she'd fallen in love with a big cattle rancher and married him in that Texas city. But he'd begun to cheat on her and she walked out to start all over again.

Whatever the reason, Clint was glad to see her again and it wasn't all due to her being a wild, wild woman in bed. He could trust Honey Bare with his life and he needed a few people like that right now, if he were to survive.

When a pretty young girl arrived and poured them hot black coffee out of a solid silver pot into fine china cups, Clint smiled. After the girl bowed and closed the door behind her, he said, "She couldn't have been more than twelve. You're not using her as one of your girls, are you?"

"Of course not! Her father and mother died of the fever this spring and she had nowhere to go. If I hadn't taken her in as my personal servant, she'd have been raped or abused and died before she was twenty. Her name is Ellen and I've sort of adopted her. When she's old enough, I think I'll send her to college."

Clint nodded. "I should have guessed it was something like that," he said a little sheepishly. "You're a good and a generous woman, Honey Bare. I'm glad that you are prospering even more than you have in the past."

They drank their coffee, each studying the other's face. It was Honey Bare who finally broke the silence between them. "I'd forgotten how good it was making love with you. Last night brought it all back in a rush. I don't know if I can ever get enough of you."

"You sure gave it a hell of a good try last night," he said with a broad grin. The woman was insatiable.

"It's more than that, though. I really would like to have you around all the time."

"Now wait a minute," he said. "I thought I explained last night about Tessa O'Grady. She needs me a whole lot worse than you do. I couldn't look myself in the mirror to shave every morning if I walked out on her before we struck gold or silver."

"And then?"

"I don't know. I've got Duke stabled in town and he'll be itching to hit the trail. Might go back up to Lake Tahoe for the rest of the summer."

"Why don't you stay here and be my man?" She took his hand. "I want you, Clint. I've had more than my share of men and you are the only one that I've seen in a good long while that I'd care to split my blanket with."

"Thanks for the compliment, but I'm not the marrying kind."

"Neither am I anymore," Honey Bare said. "I need a man like you I can love all night and trust to help me in the day."

"What kind of help?" He poured them both more coffee. "Someone like you ought to be able to afford to hire any kind of help you need for all your troubles."

"I wish that were true. But it's not. You've heard of King Cleaver, haven't you?"

Clint sat his cup down. "More than I care to. Why?"

She looked away and bit her lip. For the first time since he'd known her, Clint realized that Honey Bare was a little afraid. It came as a shock because she was a tough and hard-nosed operator when it came to business.

"Come on," he urged, "what about the man? What do you have that he could want? Do you own any mining claims or stock?"

"Nope."

"Then what?"

She stared down into her coffee almost as if she were ashamed to tell him. "Clint, he wants me. At first it was something that I just couldn't believe. He's a monster, not a man. He's so vile and..."

She shuddered so violently with revulsion that Clint put his arm around her shoulders and pulled her close.

"King always gets what he wants," Honey Bare said, "and he wants me. When huge baskets of flowers first started to arrive from California, I thought I had some secret and wealthy admirer who was also a practical enough joker to sign King's name."

"Can't fault his taste."

THE MINERS' SHOWDOWN

Tears welled up in her eyes. "It's not something to joke about! He keeps pestering me. He even has a man living with one of my best girls so that I'm watched in my own house!"

"Kick him out!"

She shook her head. "I've tried. But he's a killer. I'm afraid of him and so are all my girls."

"And you think I might be able to persuade him to go away."

"You know that's only part of it. The smallest part."

"Yeah," he said, "I do." Clint reached for his gun and holster.

"What is his name?"

"Mace Allard. He's in room eight with Taffy. She's scared to death of him." Honey Bare put her coffee down and stood to wrap her arms around Clint's neck. She hugged him tightly and whispered, "You be careful."

"That's what I told myself just a little while ago," he said, as he checked his gun and turned toward the door.

SIXTEEN

Clint moved softly down the carpeted hallway. When he came to the room, he frowned, wondering if this Mace Allard was the same man who'd tried to kill Tessa O'Grady at Lake Tahoe. Clint had wounded him that day. If so, Clint figured he'd probably have to finish what he started. Any man who'd shoot an innocent girl like Tessa, then hold another almost as a hostage, wasn't worth taking a risk to save.

He put his hand on the door and slowly tested the knob. It was locked, which came as no surprise. Clint took a deep breath and reared back. Then he kicked the door down.

Mace Allard was tall and lined with sculpted muscles. Right now he was totally occupied with the little redhead under him as his body began to spasm and jackknife in and out.

Clint watched Taffy's head roll sideways and then she stared at him in fear. Clint cocked his gun. This wasn't the same man he'd winged at Lake Tahoe but that didn't much matter anyway.

"Mace," he said, "your free ride is over. Get off the girl and get the hell out of here before I decide to make you a gelding."

THE MINERS' SHOWDOWN 81

The man coolly turned his head. He was square-jawed and ruggedly handsome and Clint had to admire his composure. Given the reverse situation, he doubted he could have handled it any better.

"So," Mace said, placing his hand on Taffy's breast and squeezing it until she cried out in pain, "I finally get to meet the famous Gunsmith."

"Let go of her and get off or I'll kill you right now."

He released Taffy, who began to cry. Then he rolled off her and stood up. He was a good six feet four and hung like a bull. Physically, he was a lot of man.

"You won't shoot," he said, reaching for his pants. "It would be cold-blooded murder and you'd hang."

Clint fired pointblank and his bullet *whanged* off Mace's belt buckle. The man jumped back, his composure shattering like a stack of dropped dishes.

"I said you'd hang!"

"Start moving for the door."

"I need my goddamn clothes!"

Clint sent a bullet between his bare feet that made him leap toward the door. "Next one," he vowed, raising his gun a little, "leaves you with nothing between your legs."

Mace slapped his hands over his crotch, whirled, and bolted into the hallway.

"Don't you ever come back, you lowdown bastard!" Taffy wailed. "Never!"

Clint stepped to the head of the stairs and saw Mace halt at the door leading into the street.

"Son of a bitch!" Mace screamed, whirling around to grab the door and wrench it open. "I'll kill you slow! I'll kill you!"

Clint raised the gun once more, knowing he was a fool not to shoot this man dead in his tracks. There was no one in this place who wouldn't swear that it was an act of self-defense.

But he couldn't do it. Just couldn't. So he put one last bullet into the floor and then Mace Allard was tearing outside, racing through a crowd of gawking men who began to hoot and jeer.

"Mister?"

Clint turned and saw Taffy coming at him with her arms

open wide. "Thank you. I owe you one hell of a favor," she breathed.

Honey Bare walked over to them. "Taffy, get back in there and rest up. Starting today, you're going to begin to earn your keep again!"

"Yes, ma'am!" But as she turned, that cute little redhead winked at Clint and made a tacit offer. Unfortunately, at a time like this, one more man-hungry woman was the last thing he needed.

Two hours later Clint climbed out of bed and dressed all over again.

"Stay," Honey Bare pleaded.

"I've got to help Tessa."

Clint pulled on his Stetson and turned to Honey. "You come visit any time you want."

"Oh, I plan to! Tessa O'Grady or no Tessa O'Grady."

Clint hurried down C Street and when he came to the Bucket of Blood Saloon he slowed and turned into the alley where he'd rolled to stop finally and shot one of his assailants. He wasn't expecting to find anything. And yet, he hoped to see a few of the kind of men who were attracted by death and who might be able to tell him that the man he'd killed was on Cleaver's payroll.

But the alley was empty. There was a wide, black stain in the dirt, and he knew it was blood. But someone had even tried to scuff that out. Clint hurried on. He shouldn't have stayed all night in Honey Bare's bed and left Tessa alone.

He marched down the hillside road passing big mining claims being worked by scores of men. Their names would fill the pages of history some day. The Belcher. Yellow Jacket. Ophir. Savage. The Consolidated Virginia. These mines were dragging out millions in ore and each had piles of tailings that rose higher than the main mast of a sailing ship.

Well, Clint thought, perhaps some day soon the Shamrock will be right up there among them as a big producer. King Cleaver and his partners certainly figured it had the potential to be one of the richest—just like their damned old Golden Eagle and some of the others that were making them a fortune.

"Tessa!" he yelled as he approached. "Tessa!"

There was no answer. He saw the tent was collapsed. Clint began to run. "Tessa!"

She was gone. He searched the machine shack—called down into the shaft, practically ripped the tent apart searching for some clue. And finally, he came upon the scribbled note that read:

> I have sold this claim to Sutro Mining and have left Comstock. I am sorry but I didn't want to run any more risks. Forgive me.
>
> Tessa

No, he thought, she wouldn't do that. Clint wadded up the note and hurled it into the sagebrush. He turned to look back up the slope of Sun Mountain toward Sutro headquarters.

He was tired of tromping up and down that hill. His head was pounding and his heart raced with fear for Tessa.

But none of that mattered. He was going back up to see King Cleaver, and this time he was going to grab that bastard by the throat and shake the truth out of him. Afterward, he was probably going to kill him for what he had done to Tessa and what he wanted to do to Honey Bare.

Two good reasons. Two damn good women.

SEVENTEEN

As the Gunsmith hurried toward C Street and the showdown he knew awaited at the headquarters of the Sutro Mining Corporation, there was a great deal on his mind. He knew with dead certainty that they'd be waiting for him and that he'd be going against a stacked deck. If he walked into King Cleaver's offices, he'd never walk out again because the place would be loaded with hired killers and he couldn't hope to outgun them all.

Getting himself killed wasn't going to help anyone, least of all himself. If Tessa were still alive, she'd be tortured until she finally broke down and signed over her claim to King. With Clint out of the picture, she'd have no hope of being rescued.

Clint reached C Street and halted on the boardwalk oblivious to the swirl of passersby. He needed to think things out a few minutes instead of just barging into the Sutro trap which he knew was waiting for him. Mace Allard would be waiting and King Cleaver would have more of his type.

I may need help if I'm to be of any good to Tessa, Clint thought grimly. This time, I can't do it alone. He changed direction and headed back down toward the Shamrock Mine. Thirty minutes later he was back and Tessa's wadded up note was smoothed out and folded in his pocket. He was going to go to the sheriff and try to convince him that Tessa had been abducted in the night and forced by the Sutro Mining Corporation to write the message.

Trouble was, Clint thought as he headed for the sheriff's office, I'm a little short of proof.

The sheriff's name was Frank Pierce and Clint had only to take one look at him to know the man wasn't going to risk his neck for anyone. He was too old and too fat to be in this line of work. Probably in his mid-sixties, Sheriff Pierce might have been a real tail-twister in his younger days.

Clint didn't have a chance to check in with him when he'd first come into town as he normally did. Things happened too quickly when he and Tessa rode in.

He was big enough, square-jawed and square shouldered. But the years had taken their toll and now the man was clearly more interested in living to see retirement than he was in stirring up a hornet's nest.

"Look," he said, handing the note to Clint and propping his feet on his desk. "You have no damned proof that girl didn't do exactly what she said she did—take the money and run. You can't go barging into the offices of the Sutro Mining Corporation and start making all those wild charges. You, better than most, ought to know that after being a lawman so many years."

Clint folded the note up and put it in his pocket. "A good lawman has to go on his instinct sometimes. You know what I'm saying. If we always waited around for proof before acting, we'd be piss-poor at our jobs."

The sheriff flushed with anger and embarrassment. "I'm not of a mind to listen to you tell me how to do my job, Gunsmith. Every man has to do things the way he sees fit."

"That's right. But he has to do his job, not just play out a role." Clint looked at the three young deputies, who studied him. These were obviously the men who kept the law in this town. They were all tough and competent in appearance; he wondered if they were honest.

"Any of you three want to join me in paying a little visit on Sutro Mining?"

Two of the three shook their heads but the third one, a young man with boyish good looks, said, "What do you plan to do when you get there? You haven't a shred of proof about Tessa. I know she wouldn't..."

"Jim!" The sheriff stood up abruptly, his eyes hard. "You stay out of this business. That's an order."

"Tessa and her father were friends. Tessa still is."

Sheriff Pierce growled, "I don't care if she is your sister, getting yourself killed wouldn't help anything."

But Jim wasn't ready to give up. "Everybody knows that King Cleaver and his crowd want the Shamrock Mine. I don't think it's any big surprise to say that we all know that Mr. O'Grady's disappearance wasn't an accident. This office didn't do a damned thing about that, either. I'm sorry, Sheriff, but I can't let them just kill Tessa and get away with that, too."

"We've no proof of anything!"

"Then maybe we ought to start digging for some," Jim said stubbornly. "Sheriff, I wouldn't work for you if I didn't know you were a good and honest man. You are fixing to retire this winter. I don't blame you for turning your head on this, but I plan to be around for a good long while, and I can't let this slide by any longer."

He stepped up to the sheriff. "I'm going with the Gunsmith. I've a question or two of my own to ask and then I'm going to start looking for Tessa. If you want, I'll give you my badge so there will be no trouble brought to you."

He started to unpin it but the sheriff waved his hand and snapped, "Leave it on, Jim. You're too good a man to lose. We all know you're the best one to fill my place. I just think you're getting into something that is way over your head. If the Gunsmith had any real proof, I'd march to Sutro myself. But he doesn't."

Clint stepped forward. "And I never will until I start rattling their cages. Tessa O'Grady is still alive. I'm certain of it. But we have to find her soon."

The sheriff scowled fiercely, but after a moment, he reached into his desk drawer and pulled out his gun and holster and strapped it around his potbelly.

"Damn it," he groused, "I'm too old and slow to be in this job. But the only way I'm going to keep you both from getting blown apart is to let King Cleaver know I'm behind you."

"You want us to come?" another deputy asked.

The sheriff looked at his other two deputies. "Naw," he said, "You two go patrol the saloons and haul in a few drunks. Judge says we need more fines if my damned retirement is to amount to anything more than beer and bean money."

They both smiled and left.

"I appreciate this," Clint said to the sheriff and his young deputy.

"We're not doing it for you," Pierce rumbled. "Tessa O'Grady and her father were fine people. We liked them both."

Clint nodded. He understood but he sure didn't like the way the sheriff said "were" and spoke of them both as if they were dead. Maybe Jim didn't either because as they left the office, his expression was as bleak as a Montana prairie in January.

Clint couldn't help but wonder if either one of them knew something he did not.

EIGHTEEN

Sheriff Pierce went in first and it was a good thing that he did because he came face to face with a crowd of gunmen. Clint followed the young deputy and, for a moment, the atmosphere was crackling with tension.

The sheriff looked at the faces of at least a dozen armed men and said, "Mace, go get your boss and tell him to get out here pronto."

Mace's eyes were locked with those of the Gunsmith. Clint had never seen anyone with so much hatred boiling right at the surface. He thought Mace would be crazy enough to draw and everyone else be damned. And maybe, if the sheriff hadn't distracted him, he would have.

"Mace!" The sheriff stepped between them. "Go tell Cleaver to come out here before you do or say something that will get you killed."

Clint glanced at the sheriff. There was more than a passing hint of familiarity between him and the half-crazed gunfighter. It made him wonder.

Mace finally pulled himself under tight control and spun on

his heel. He moved so jerkily that it was as if he were being pulled by wires. Clint figured that was good, because when the day came that he'd have to face the man's gun, he wanted him to be too eager, too throttled by hatred to make a smooth draw.

They waited for less than a minute before King Cleaver waddled out.

"What do you want, Sheriff?" he asked with annoyance, studying the Gunsmith. "You know I do not appreciate interruptions."

To Pierce's credit, he did not rattle. His voice stayed cool and steady. "I know that you and Clint Adams have already met and that there is no love lost between you. But he has a few questions that my deputy would also like to know the answers to."

King actually smiled then. "All right, Sheriff. I am a law-abiding citizen—a cooperative man who generously funds civic needs and supports elected officials. Let's hear the questions."

Clint was watching the sheriff. It was clear that King's message had registered—if the sheriff wanted any political help in receiving a more generous retirement, he'd damn well better remember who helped fund his last election campaign. Clint had seen it all before. Sheriffs never earned what they were worth and most all of them were beholden to the generosity of prominent and prosperous civic leaders. In Virginia City, this was obviously quite true.

Clint unfolded the note and handed it to Cleaver who glanced at it, then looked up and hissed, "So?"

"So you and the Sutro Mining Corporation are after that claim and have been all along. I want to know who bought it."

"How should I know? We didn't."

"But you will," Clint said. "Unless I miss my guess, either you did buy it or one of your men bought it and will sell it to you when the smoke clears."

"Pure supposition, Adams." He turned to the sheriff. "I don't have to put up with this man's ridiculous and slanderous theories."

Clint reached out and grabbed Cleaver by the arm and pulled

him around. "What have you done with Tessa?" he asked in a soft yet deadly voice. "Where is she?"

"I don't know what you are talking about!"

Clint stared into those cold reptilian eyes, and something snapped inside of him; he jumped for King's throat. Both the deputy and Sheriff Pierce had been expecting it and they grabbed him and pulled him back.

"Arrest that man!" King screamed. "Arrest him!"

The deputy held Clint and he shouted, "Clint, this won't help things!"

Clint relaxed. Jim was right. If he had grabbed King by the throat, then the sheriff would have had no choice but to arrest him for assault. "Thanks," he whispered.

Clint looked at King Cleaver. "You have her," he said. "I know it and so does every other man in this room. And I'll find her and then we'll see who goes to jail. Kidnapping is a pretty serious offense. It will send you to prison and you won't survive a week among those men."

"You bore me," King said, almost yawning as he stepped up to Clint until his face was inches away. "You can't hurt me at all."

Clint stepped back and then spun around and headed outside. King was doing everything in his power to provoke an assault and he had almost succeeded. From now on, Clint thought, I can't trust myself to get near the man. I'll have to find Tessa on my own.

A few minutes later the sheriff and his deputy came out. Jim looked troubled. "Adams, you almost swam into his net."

"I know it. Won't happen again."

"Better not," the sheriff warned. "If you kill him or Mace, odds are that you'll swing. Might be best if you just climb on that big horse of yours and ride off the Comstock and keep going."

"And leave Tessa?"

"Maybe she has already left you, Gunsmith." The sheriff started back toward his office.

Clint turned to the deputy. "You don't believe that, do you?"

Jim scuffed the dirt with the toe of his boot. "No," he said finally, "I don't believe it for a minute. But then, I'm not always right about things either. I don't know Tessa as well as I sure want to. Fact is, I didn't know her very well at all. We talked a few times on the street. After her father disappeared, I tried to help find him. Never had any luck."

"But you are suspicious of King Cleaver, aren't you?"

"Damn right. I still think King had old O'Grady murdered and then pitched down some mine shaft or buried out in the desert. But no one will ever know for certain."

"He wouldn't have left his daughter sitting on a gold mine," Clint argued.

"How much did Tessa tell you about her father?"

Clint blinked. "Not much. Why?"

"No reason she'd want to, Adams. You see, he was loco. He and his best friend, Scotty Herman prospected all over the California gold fields together. Neither one of them ever had any luck and they both suffered and scraped for years. Finally, they came to Nevada Territory and prospected."

"What has this got to do with Tessa?"

Jim shrugged. "Maybe something, maybe nothing. The point of it is that he and Scotty came up here and rumor has it they struck it rich. They went back to California to get some financing because they both knew that it would take lots of money to work this mountainside. But only one man came back from that trip to stake his legal claim."

"O'Grady."

"That's right," Jim said quietly. "It was almost six months before Scotty showed up, and when he did he looked more dead than alive. I had to stop them from going to war. They hated each other. Scotty never talked about it too much when he was sober. But I threw him in jail drunk enough times to hear the story a bunch of times. O'Grady and Scotty got into an argument on the way back from California and they had a gunfight. O'Grady left his friend for dead in a Sierra blizzard. When Scotty showed up, O'Grady sort of went crazy and tried to drink himself to death."

"Why didn't he just give half the Shamrock Mine to Scotty?"

"I don't know. Maybe it was because of Tessa. It doesn't

matter anymore, I guess. Reason I'm telling you this is that there are a lot of folks who believe that Scotty killed O'Grady—King Cleaver is innocent."

The deputy took a deep breath. "I'm not so sure Scotty didn't do it. He got crazy there towards the last. I always thought that they might just as well have killed each other over in California. After they came back here, neither one of them was ever the same."

Clint shook his head. "Tessa never said anything about any Scotty Herman. Just King Cleaver."

"If your father did that to his best friend and partner, maybe you wouldn't want to tell anybody about it, either."

"So where does all this put us?" Clint asked. "You don't think that Scotty would have hurt Tessa, do you?"

"Scotty goes crazy when he drinks too much. The only thing that keeps him alive is that he loves his burro Daisy so damned much. He'd have shot himself long ago if he thought she'd be taken care of after his death. With a man like that, nothing surprises me. I'm not saying that Scotty took Tessa away, but it is something to think about."

Clint shook his head. "I wish Duke and I were back up at Lake Tahoe. This whole thing is getting worse by the minute."

"Sure it is," the deputy said. "If it were simple and straightforward, don't you think I'd have stepped in and solved the mystery myself?"

"Yeah," Clint said, "I believe you would have. Where can I find Scotty?"

"I don't know. But when you find him . . . be careful. He's crazy like a fox. One minute you think he's just a pathetic old man who has drunk too much liquor and is killing himself; the next minute you look into his bloodshot eyes and you swear he's going to kill you if you drop your guard for an instant. In a lot of ways, I think he's even more dangerous than someone like Mace Allard who stands there and dares you to draw on him."

"You ever seen him draw on anyone?"

"Nope. Lots of folks have, though. They say he's the fastest ever. Faster even than the Gunsmith."

Clint said nothing. He'd heard that many, many times and

it had never been true. But it would be some day and perhaps that day and place was here—and soon.

"Adams?"

"Yeah?"

"I can't help you very much. I'm being paid to patrol the streets—to keep drunk miners from being rolled and beaten. And there is another thing—I mean to be the sheriff here come the election this winter."

"Does that mean you need King Cleaver and his Sutro Mining?"

The deputy thought about that for a little while before he answered. "It means that I will if he's still in business."

Clint nodded. "I see," he said, but he did not really see at all. The deputy seemed to be straddling the fence, ready to go either way depending on what happened. If Clint had evidence to put King Cleaver behind bars, then the deputy would help—but if not, he'd just as easily turn the other way.

"I appreciate your help," Clint said. "But I'm not going to count on it."

"Best that you don't," the deputy advised. "I'm telling you honest and straight to your face that it is best that you don't."

The man walked away then and Clint just shook his head. He wasn't any nearer to finding Tessa than he had been two hours ago, and now the mystery of her disappearance was even deeper than he'd first thought.

Instead of just Tessa, he also had a crazy old miner to find. And for some reason, his lawman's instincts told him time was running short.

NINETEEN

Clint covered every saloon on the Comstock asking the whereabouts of Scotty Herman. No one had seen him in at least a week and most of the bartenders were hoping they never, ever saw him again. From what he heard, Clint was able to get a good picture of the old prospector and it wasn't a pretty one. Scotty was a big man, well over six feet tall, and still strong enough to bust up a bar and raise considerable hell.

Everyone agreed he was a smart old bastard, cunning and shrewd, and one of the most knowledgeable men on the Comstock. When Clint asked why Scotty, if he were so good, had never again found a strike, the bartenders all said the same thing. Scotty would rather drink than work, rather fight than bother to file a promising strike. He would work a claim until it finally began to pay off; then he'd take his newfound earnings and blow them on the town, buying everyone drinks until all his money was gone. When that happened, he'd sell his new strike to the highest bidder for another few hundred dollars and start a whole new round of drinking until he was broke again.

But although he'd sell his claim for whiskey, he'd never

THE MINERS' SHOWDOWN

part with the little Mexican burro he loved so much. He fed Daisy the best flour, sugar and molasses that money could buy and often lovingly talked about taking the little burro out into the valleys of Nevada where the grass was tall and rich. If there was any joy at all in Scotty's life, it was due to Daisy. Everybody agreed that after he and old O'Grady had had their falling out, the only thing that Scotty gave a damn about was Daisy.

Almost the only thing. One bartender did say that Scotty cared deeply about Tessa, said Scotty wished he'd had a daughter like her himself. He'd been very drunk that night, though, and Scotty lied a lot.

So where had the old prospector gone? And would he be able to help the Gunsmith? These were tough questions and the last thing Clint wanted to do was go chasing some old devil who might not be able to give him the slightest clue. But Scotty was his only lead outside of going sneaking into the Sutro headquarters and King Cleaver's mansion.

By nightfall, Clint was convinced that Scotty Herman was not in town but had probably taken Daisy down to the Carson River meadows to graze.

Clint knew he had to break into the Sutro offices and search them and if Tessa wasn't found he'd go up to King's mansion and search that. If he still hadn't found the young woman, he'd have no choice but to ride on down to the Carson River and hunt up old Scotty.

He went to the stable and saddled Duke. The big horse was happy to see him and plenty eager to get out of its stall. He looked good though, fatter than when he'd arrived, and his coat was slick and shiny from brushing. Clint was pleased that he'd paid for the extra care and tipped handsomely.

When he swung into the saddle, it felt good. Duke danced with eagerness and he rode down C Street for about a mile, then pulled in at a hitching post and tied the horse up beside several others. Duke swung his head around and it was obvious that he was not pleased.

"Don't worry," Clint said. "I got a hunch we'll be doing a whole lot more riding before the night is up. Nothing good has happened to me yet up here—correction, I forgot about Honey

Bare. You probably remember her." Honey Bare had fed Duke too many apples, the poor horse, and she'd also nearly ruined him on sugar candy.

"Be back soon," he said, patting the gelding.

It was no trick at all to get into the Sutro offices. There were locks on the doors, but Clint had learned how to pick them for occasions just like this. A man who understood the intricate workings of guns sure as hell wasn't going to be stymied by a lock.

The inside of the headquarters was very dark. Clint pulled his gun and moved through the foyer and then into King Cleaver's office. Empty. He spent a half hour rummaging through King's files hoping to find something in writing about the Shamrock Mine. He came up empty, though; that wasn't surprising because a man as rich and powerful as King was way too smart to leave any incriminating evidence lying around. If there were any records, they'd be locked in some vault, probably in the Bank of Virginia City where no one could get to them. Satisfied that he was wasting his time, Clint hurried through the other offices and then left the building by the same door he'd come in through, locking it again. When he rode away, there was no evidence that he'd been inside.

King Cleaver lived in a big hilltop mansion to the north of town. The mansion was of gothic design; it was a monstrosity that perfectly characterized its owner's hideous and perverse tastes. King had painted it pink with bright red trim. The mansion hung on the top of the hill and seemed to gloat like some smug know-it-all.

It was a two-story affair with lots of ribbed vaulting, a flying buttress that seemed to go nowhere, and pointed arches and rooftops built more to impress than to serve any useful purpose. Some of the miners thought it was beautiful, but then after a few years of living in a cave, a man could not be faulted if his sense of taste corroded.

Clint wasn't interested in whether or not the house was ugly, but he did care about its being guarded twenty-four hours a day. It was said that King lived in the mansion all alone except for his servants, cooks, and Chinese boys. People knew for a fact that his guards and hired gunmen slept in a separate building that was designed and built as the stable. Maybe it was King's way of stating how he felt about such hirelings.

A half mile from the pink mansion, Clint dismounted in an empty gully choked with sagebrush.

"I wish there were some covering trees I could hide you in, Duke, but there's damn few of them around these parts and I want you close in case I need you in a hurry."

He started up the gully, knowing it would take him up past the mansion and that any guards would be watching mainly the lower road. The going was tough and it was difficult keeping his footing because of all the rocks he had to thread his way over.

When Clint guessed he was finally above the mansion, he eased up to the lip of the gully and peered up at the gothic nightmare. The upstairs lights were still on and he studied the windows in some futile hope that he might see Tessa or hear her voice.

The night wore on. Clint watched the stars come out and he could hear coyotes howl off in the hills somewhere. He hoped that Tessa was still alive and could hear them, too. The realization that he might be too late to save her filled him with dread. He grew impatient, and when the lights finally blinked out, he was ready to move.

He made it to the porch and slipped inside with no problem whatsoever. The entrance was impressive with big marble statues lined up against the walls and he passed through an enormous parlor into a great living room decorated with exotic Oriental rugs and statuary and paintings that he could not see very well. He smelled incense and the smoke of opium and he heard either a woman or a child coughing in some room upstairs.

Clint moved with care for he had decided that he did not want to risk detection unless he had Tessa in his arms. To get caught or in a gunfight before finding her would be stupid and futile. If he were captured, he would go to prison, and *that* was the best thing that could happen—the alternative was death, probably by torture.

Within minutes he had covered the entire downstairs. Clint

arrived at the stairs and started placing each boot down as carefully as he could. Luckily, they were carpeted and very solid; they did not creak as he mounted them one by one.

At the top of the staircase, he stood, gun in hand, and tried to guess which room deserved his most urgent attention. He did not have to remind himself that the risk of detection was very high. Downstairs, he'd avoided the rooms which were obviously the cook's, maid's, and butler's quarters. Upstairs, it was going to be a little more difficult. If Tessa were here, she would most likely be upstairs, not down.

The first bedroom was empty and so was the second. But in the third, he could feel a human's presence and he moved on tiptoe across the rich Oriental carpet until he stared down at the faces of two young Chinese boys. In sleep they looked like a pair of porcelain dolls, so innocent and perfect. Clint's jaw muscles corded and he quickly left the room. He had a mean, angry expression on his face when he entered the hallway; any man who favored children over women was deserving of a bullet through the brain.

Never mind the fact that King wanted Honey Bare, he was still keeping boys for his pleasure and that alone made Clint think he ought to be strung up, then shot.

There were two more bedrooms and one of them was empty and the other held King. Clint could hear the man snoring and he moved in to see him. King was lying in a huge hand-carved four-poster with the covers thrown back.

Beside him was another small boy, and when Clint moved to the bed, the child stirred and softly whimpered.

Clint froze. The China boy's eyes fluttered open and, for an instant, he stared at the ceiling. He was almost beautiful, no older than twelve, small, and especially delicate.

Seeing him lying beside this great beast brought into Clint's mouth a low choke of hatred that he could not swallow.

The boy looked right at him and screamed in fright.

"Shhhhhh!" Clint brought his finger up to his lips and drew his gun. The boy ducked under the covers and kept screaming even though his voice was muffled.

King was a heavy sleeper but he'd have had to have been dead not to awaken. Clint saw him start and his eyes flew open as he tried to focus and react. Clint gave him time to do neither. He pistol-whipped him across the forehead, then punched him hard up and under the jaw. King just groaned and went limp.

The Chinese boy was still wailing but Clint paid him no mind because other voices were already ringing through the mansion. Frightened and angry voices. Clint rushed to the window and peered down toward the stables.

Lights were going on there. In a minute or less the place would be swarming with gunmen. It was time to get the hell off this hillside—if it wasn't already too late.

TWENTY

Clint dashed out into the hallway and sprinted down to the last empty bedroom. He heard shouts from below as he closed the door behind him and locked it. Then he rushed to the window and threw it open. The rooftop was steep and wet with dew and he damned near slipped getting through the window. But he managed to hang on to the sill and keep his balance, then crawl down the roof until he reached a small gable.

He could hear shouts now and men racing up the stairway. Clint lay down on the roof and allowed his body to slide down the steep rooftop until his toes dropped over the edge. He dug his fingernails into the shingles and hung on for all he was worth.

But his legs slipped over the edge and he'd have sailed off if it hadn't been for his gunbelt's being caught on some protruding nails.

"Damn!" he whispered, dangling on the edge and trying desperately to extricate himself from this miserable predicament. He had two choices; he could either hang by his belt until someone noticed his legs dangling over the rooftop, or he could tear himself free and drop to the earth hoping he didn't land on someone or break his legs.

He chose the latter alternative and twisted violently sideways. He pulled free and his body resumed its slide. Clint did manage to grab the roof's edge at the very last moment and he hung there trying to see what was below him. Seeing nothing but sage, he let go.

It felt as if he dropped a hundred feet instead of only twenty. When he hit, the sage acted like a cushion, but it whipped his legs out from under him and then as he crashed through the branches, it scraped the hell out of his arms and put a nasty cut along one cheek.

Clint didn't have time to assess the damages. He stood up shakily but without any broken bones or twisted ankles. He pulled out his gun and blew it clean, and then he charged ahead just as a gunshot exploded in the night.

"There he is!"

Clint glanced back. He could see silhouettes, nothing more, and knew they could not have recognized him. He fired two shots and the pursuers dived for cover. Clint turned and ran into the night. A quarter mile away, he angled back toward the gully.

Duke snorted encouragement and Clint wasted no time in swinging up into the saddle and racing away. He could hear shouts and curses from the hilltop and even an occasional burst of gunfire.

There were a lot of angry men back there, and though they might suspect it was him, the only one who'd seen him at all was that poor China boy—and King Cleaver would have one hell of a time using him as a witness. No, Clint thought, this was one time when lack of evidence was going to work in his favor.

He rode back through Virginia City and then over the Divide and down into Gold Hill and Silver City. At the latter, he stopped long enough to ask a few questions in the saloons. Had anyone seen the girl Tessa O'Grady pass through? What about old Scotty Herman?

The answers were no and yes. Scotty was down on the

Carson River with his burro and, with any luck at all, maybe he'd get bit by a rattlesnake and die, thus providing the entire Comstock a good reason for celebration.

Clint thanked them for the information and rode on. Morning found him galloping through the sage toward the line of cottonwood trees that always marked a Nevada river or stream. He wasn't sure how far he'd have to travel to find the irascible old prospector, but he figured it wouldn't be too great a distance. Everyone admitted that Scotty was a man who did not enjoy exercise except when it involved bending his elbow at the bar.

All along the river Clint saw big sawmills. Twenty miles away on the eastern slopes of the Sierra Nevada mountains, whole forests were being chopped down. Trees were shorn of their branches, cut into manageable lengths, then they were floated down the river.

When Clint rode through the little logging settlement of Empire City, he saw great booms reaching out to lift timber from the Carson River and swing it into the hungry maws of the sawmills where it was cut for mine timbering or new construction, then stacked to dry and be delivered on the Comstock. It was said that there were entire forests buried under Virginia City, and watching all this early morning activity, Clint guessed that was probably true. Besides the great amount of timber needed underground, all the hoisting works operated on steam engines and the fires burned day and night.

"Have you seen an old prospector with a mule pass by?" he kept asking.

"You mean that crusty old sumbitch, Scotty?"

"That's the one," he'd answer.

"Saw him upriver yesterday afternoon. He was fishing and drinking. Raising hell with some loggers."

Clint kept riding and at about nine o'clock in the morning he finally saw the prospector sitting out in the river on a logjam yelling obscenities at some men for ruining his favorite fishing hole.

Clint frowned. He dismounted and let Duke graze near the speckled mule, then went to see this man he'd heard so many stories about.

THE MINERS' SHOWDOWN

"Hello!" Clint shouted, not eager to make his way out on to the logjam. "Can you come here and talk?"

Scotty cussed him for a few minutes. He was a tall, slightly bent man with a big rack of shoulders and wild gray hair. His beard was salt and pepper, and he wore a shapeless old black hat that was pulled low over his eyes.

"I need to talk to you!" Clint yelled over the river sound.

"Then get your ass out here!" Scotty grinned with wicked pleasure. "That is if you've balls enough to do it!"

Clint took a deep breath and had a few choice words of his own to offer. But Scotty was a contrary old bastard and he'd stay out there all day if he thought somebody wanted him to come ashore. Clint figured he had no choice but to walk the logs.

The first log he stepped on bobbed a little and that threw him off balance so that he lurched out onto the jam, arms windmilling furiously, Scotty roaring with laughter.

Clint stepped about twenty feet before a log rolled under his foot and he fell, sprawling. He lay there staring at the dirty water and listening to old Scotty roar. Clint pushed himself up shakily and drew his gun. Even as Scotty's mouth crimped down in puzzlement and then fright, Clint took aim and shot the hat off his head.

Scotty reared back and roared in anger. "Damn you!" he shouted, jumping up and down in a fury and then starting toward Clint like a man intent on murder. "I'll beat the hell out of you!"

Clint jumped to his feet, retreated to the safety of the riverbank, and let Scotty come ashore. "That's far enough, you crazy old coot," he warned, "or my next bullet is going to be six inches lower and right between your eyes."

Scotty was trying to tear a young cottonwood tree out of the ground to use on Clint. But the warning brought him up short. He kicked the resisting tree in anger and then turned to face Clint, his bloodshot eyes glued to the gun.

"Who are you and what do you want?"

"I'm a friend of Tessa O'Grady's," Clint said. "I'm trying to help her hang on to the Shamrock Mine."

All the belligerence drained out of his whiskey-ruined, old

face. "Tessa come back? Thought they killed her already."

"Uh-uh," Clint said. "They tried to up at Lake Tahoe but I got in their way. Now, they've taken her away and I can't find her. I hoped you might know where I could look."

Scotty's head drooped and he stared down at his mud-crusted boots. "I liked Tessa," he whispered. "She was a good girl. Used to carry her on these shoulders of mine when she was a young'un over near Sutter's Mill. She and I, we picked flowers and sweet grass for Daisy. Daisy never let anyone ride her 'cept Tessa. I liked Tessa. She was O'Grady's little girl, but she was mine, too."

Right there and then Clint knew that all the rumors that it was Scotty who'd killed O'Grady and maybe even had caused Tessa trouble were false. "You know where I might find her?"

He didn't look up and Clint had to strain to hear him over the river. "Cemetery or down some empty mine shaft most likely."

Clint swallowed. "That's all? I thought . . . thought maybe there was some place she might have run to hide if she was in trouble. Maybe they didn't take her away but she knew they were coming and just had to clear out until it was safe to come back."

Scotty looked up at him. His eyes were bleary and watered. He looked terrible. "King, he wants that mine and he took it. Killed O'Grady. Took our Shamrock and is gutting it right now."

"We could stop him," Clint said, unable to hide the hope and the urgency he felt. "I could use your help. You see, I don't know a damn thing about mining. There's machinery there that doesn't work but I have enough money to fix it. I just need some directions. But first, I need to find Tessa if she's still alive."

"She ain't!" Scotty straightened and his bloodless lips twisted in anger.

"How do you know!" Clint yelled. "You can't be sure. Not until we find her." He lowered his voice. "Listen, Scotty. I know you've given up on everything. But I haven't and neither has Tessa. If she's alive, I intend to find her and save her. Now, one last time before I go, do you have any idea? Any idea at all where I can hunt? I already went through the Sutro offices and King Cleaver's mansion. She wasn't there and I don't know where else to look and I swear I'll flatten you if you tell me to quit or look for fresh graves in the cemetery."

Scotty dragged the back of his blue-veined hand across his mouth. "You got any whiskey in those saddlebags?"

"I bought a bottle for you in Silver City," Clint told him. "But I'm not going to just hand it over to you until you at least try to help me."

Scotty watched his burro graze in the meadow for a long time and Clint was about ready to walk away in disgust when the old man said, "I knew a man once who had a fox come visit his henhouse."

Clint waited. And waited. "So?"

"Smartest fox you ever heard of, it was. Every couple of nights it would raid and he'd come runnin' out with his shotgun to kill it, but it always just got away. He set traps. Set up all night, too. Fox kept takin' a chicken. Always killed just one and ate it nearby."

Clint was in no mood for long-winded stories. "Did the man ever catch the fox?"

"Nope." Scotty scratched his beard. "Fox ate all his chickens right down to the very last one. Farmer didn't care though 'cause he finally figured out how the fox did it."

"How?"

"Fox lived way up inside the chicken house where you couldn't see him. He musta liked to keep it neat so he always dug out and traveled a ways before he ate his feathered friends. Ate every one of them and then he moved on."

Clint heaved a sigh of exasperation. "I don't see what in the hell that has to do with solving the problem."

Scotty smiled with a crafty look in his watery, old eyes and chuckled, "Neither did the farmer."

Clint was furious but he gave the old prospector the whiskey anyway before he galloped back toward the Comstock. It would be afternoon before he could reach Virginia City and he'd have wasted a night and most of a day and be no closer to discovering where Tessa might be.

Damn old windbag!

• • •

He rode hard over the Divide, and just as the sweeping panorama of the Comstock Lode opened up before him, so did the meaning of Scotty's fox-in-the-henhouse story.

"Come on, Duke!" he shouted. "I think I know where to find her. I just hope she's alive!"

TWENTY-ONE

Clint cursed himself for not having figured it out without Scotty's help. Now that he realized that it would have been impossible to carry Tessa off her claim and Comstock without someone noticing, it was so obvious that they must have sent her down the Shamrock mine. The question was whether or not they lowered her tied and bound or threw her down to a certain death.

He raced along the dirt roads until he came to the Shamrock and then he called out her name. There was no answer, but he hadn't expected one.

Clint moved very quickly now. In the machine shed tucked under the steam engine that drove the hoisting reel was a big coil of stout hemp rope. Clint dug it out and tied it around a piece of machinery and lowered it into the shaft. He scrambled back to the tent and stuffed matches and candles into his coat pockets and then he slung a canteen over his shoulder. He was ready.

It was scary just crawling over the lip of that round hole and wondering if the rope he'd thrown down had reached bottom. If it hadn't, he'd have to climb back up and get some help. And maybe he should have done that anyway but he was in too big a hurry and he couldn't be sure that Tessa was down there—it just made sense that she might be.

Clint took a deep breath and went over the side, winding his legs around the heavy rope and using his arms to keep from going down too fast. The shaft was inside under cover from the elements. Maybe if it had been out in the open and the sun were directly overhead he might have been able to see the bottom, but maybe doesn't count for much and it was totally dark after he'd lowered himself twenty feet. And surprisingly, the air immediately started to get warmer.

"Tessa," he whispered, "are you down here?"

There wasn't a sound except for the pebbles falling off the sides of the shaft whenever he bumped into it. Clint kept sliding deeper and deeper until he began to wonder just how much longer the rope would hold and if it were long enough to reach the bottom.

Just about the time he became convinced that it wasn't going to be, his boots touched a hard rock and he sighed with relief. "Tessa!"

He struck a match and the cavern glowed faintly before the match died. "Damn it!" Clint swore, lighting another. "Tessa!"

He saw her; she was propped against the wall of the cavern no more than twenty feet away. She was facing him and was both gagged and blindfolded.

Clint sprang towards her and his sudden motion blew out the candle, but he did not care as he groped his way to her side and took her in his arms. He tore off her gag and blindfold and pulled her close.

"Oh, Clint!" she whispered in a dry, cracked voice. "I was beginning to think you'd never come down here and find me!"

"Hadn't have been for old Scotty Herman, I never would have, Tessa." He untied her, gave her the canteen, and then listened to her drink while he fumbled for the matches and the candles.

When he lit one, he saw her blink and shield her eyes for a moment. Clint studied her closely. "Are you all right?"

"I will be once I get out of here," she said, looking up toward a distant circle of light that looked like a bead of silver. "You don't have any idea how much I prayed you'd hurry and find me."

Clint raised the candle and studied the cavern. It was fairly large, about the size of a one-room log cabin. It reminded Clint of the inside of a hollowed pumpkin and he could see the beginnings of tunnels leading off in all four directions on the compass. But the one going to the west toward the depths of Sun Mountain was by far the biggest. It pushed back out of the cavern a good thirty feet and ended at a rock face.

Clint rose to his feet and walked to a lantern hanging from the timbering. He lit it and blew out the candle. "Your father do all of this?"

"Yes. He believed that he'd strike gold to the west. He never did."

Clint returned to sit beside Tessa. "Did you see who did this to you."

She shook her head. "I was waiting for you, Clint. Sometime in the night I fell asleep and the next thing I knew men were throwing a blanket over my head and I was being lifted and carried out of the tent. I tried to yell but they clamped something over my mouth and I almost suffocated."

"How did they get you down here?"

"Tied a rope around my waist and lowered me. Then some of them came down. I was blindfolded in the dark; then my ankles were tied together."

"Did you recognize any of their voices?"

"No." She swallowed noisily. Tears sprang to her eyes. "They told me what to write on a note. I wouldn't do it so they started to unbutton my nightshirt..."

Clint ground his teeth in anger.

"I couldn't see but I could hear and one of them started to untie my ankles saying he was going to have the first turn at raping me. I guess I went crazy when they started to pull my legs apart and when I stopped screaming into the gag I passed out."

"The rotten bastards!"

Tessa nodded weakly. "The next thing I knew was that they were pouring water in my face and it was going up my nose and I was choking so bad I thought I was going to drown. They just kept pouring the water and finally... finally I let them know that I would write whatever they wanted if they'd leave me be."

"Did they?" he asked.

Tessa looked away. "All but one," she whispered. "He told the others to go on up the rope and that he would be along. They didn't want to but he made them. Then, when they were gone he... he..."

Clint put his fingers to her bruised lips. "That's all right, Tessa. It's over. I won't leave you again until it's finished with all of them. I promise."

She nodded. "Clint?"

"Yes?"

"He was tall, lean, and strong and he had puckered scar."

"Where?"

She reached down and placed a finger just to the right of Clint's belt buckle. "Here," she told him quietly. "I could feel it all the time he was doing it to me."

Clint nodded. He wondered if it was Mace Allard or not. Mace was tall and strong, but Clint couldn't remember if he'd had a big scar on his lower abdomen. Maybe it didn't matter so much anyway because he knew full well he was already going to have to kill the man. But when he did, he was going to check and see.

"Tessa, I know how rough this has been, perhaps you should sell the mine. I'm certain I could find a buyer who is not afraid of the Sutro Mining Corporation. There are a lot of big operations up here and King Cleaver doesn't own them all."

"No."

"Are you absolutely sure? I can't guarantee that I can stop them all."

She pulled him close and held him tightly. "I don't want a guarantee, Clint. I just want us to give it our best shot. That's all I ask."

TWENTY-TWO

No one on the entire Comstock would sell replacement parts to Clint and Tessa for the Shamrock Mine. After three infuriating days of going from machinery dealer to machinery dealer, Clint finally left Virginia City and found a man in Carson City who was able to find some used parts. Clint paid the man well for not only delivering them but also for making sure they fit and worked.

Like most mines on the Comstock, a steam engine was used to raise and lower a wire cage containing men, equipment, and the ore that was worked each day along with the low-grade stuff that formed the huge tailings near the shaft of every deep mine.

Clint had listened enough to the miners to realize that the ore was not in a single and defined vein, but was found in little pockets here and there, almost like raisins in a pudding or cake. If a man got lucky, he punched through the often soft sheets of clay and struck it rich. He could almost scoop the ore out like mud and it would yield in excess of three thousand dollars a ton, and a single man could remove a ton a day if he had the machinery to back him.

Clint now had that machinery, and when the boiler reached the proper temperature and the steam built to the critical level to give their little engine power, he dared to step on to the cage and grip the twisted wire mine cable.

It took some effort to keep his voice steady but he managed. "You ever lower your father down on this thing?"

Tessa grabbed the control throttle and the handle of the winch. "Don't you worry," she told him, "I have no intention of making a mistake. But hang on, this first step is a dilly."

It was meant to be a joke, only Clint was in no mood. So he nodded he was ready and hung on with both hands. Tessa took the controls and pulled the handle.

He dropped like a stone for the first twenty feet and his heart seemed to fill his throat. Clint hung on and figured it was all over for him, but the cage's brake caught and it shuddered to a crawl.

Clint looked up at the circle of light and shook his head. He knew he should have let Tessa practice a few more times.

But he made it to the bottom and found his lantern. The cavern, which they called a station in the bigger mines, had a good supply of tools, blasting powder, and fuses. Trouble was, Clint knew damn little about using any of it. And since the Comstock was notorious for cave-ins, he decided he'd just stick with the hand tools and leave the blasting powder for another time when he had some expert help.

He picked up the tools and moved west along the longest tunnel, or drift, until he came to a wall. It was scarred with pick marks and had obviously been the choice of O'Grady.

"Well," Clint said, spitting on his hands and grabbing his pick, "I guess if this was where O'Grady thought it best to dig, then I might as well go along."

Without further hesitation, Clint planted his feet and set to work.

That evening he had Tessa bring him back up and he was so tired he could barely move. Every muscle in his body was on fire and in torment.

Tessa went out in search of some liniment and came back with a jar of it.

"It burns!" Clint swore, pushing himself up on his elbows and glaring at her. "What is that stuff?"

He grabbed the bottle and stared at it suspiciously. "Horse liniment!"

"That was all I could find," Tessa said. "Besides, the old miner I got it from said they all use it for stiff and sore muscles. Said to put some of it on the palms of your hands so they won't blister."

Clint stared at his hands. They were a mass of blisters. "Too damn late for that now," he groused.

Tessa kept rubbing the liniment into his back and working her way down until she was rubbing it into his buttocks. "Don't hurt there, girl."

She giggled and began to unbutton her blouse. "There's only about one area of your whole body that's probably still up to snuff, might as well take advantage of it, Clint."

She was rubbing the horse liniment where it wasn't meant to be rubbed and Clint flopped back and had no mind to tell her to stop. Sometimes a man just had to give in a little, even at the risk of his own health.

During the days and then the weeks that followed, his hands became tough and his screaming muscles lost their voices. Clint worked like a demon on the west wall and Tessa worked almost as hard up above operating the lift cage, then unloading it and sorting out the promising ore and loading it into a wagon to be sent to the assayer's office.

Every night they figured they must have found some paydirt and yet about noon the next day came the assayer's report that they had not. They still were searching, still looking for one of those ore bodies that in some mines were reaching depths of nearly two thousand feet.

Tessa was worried and too tried to hide her concern. She had risked her life as well as Clint's in this gamble and she was certain that her father had not been mistaken when he'd promised that the ore was down there somewhere. But where? How deep? With Clint practically killing himself all alone, it might take ten years to strike an ore body. She knew he would not wait that long. Not ten years or ten months or even ten weeks. He wasn't a miner but he was doing his damn level best for them.

Sometimes near the end of the day she would make him come up early and then she'd go down and work the face of the west wall for a few hours. It made her realize how brutally hard it was and why miners drank so savagely during their leisure.

Down in the mine a person lost track of night and day. Time lost all meaning. A miner just stood and swung his pick and pulled rock down and prayed that the ceiling didn't cave in.

Sometimes it did. Tessa quickly developed a miner's instincts for when the rock was unstable and then she worked with one eye ahead and one eye pointed up. Rock usually didn't just drop; it began to crack along the ceiling and then it made a grinding sound in warning. If you didn't listen, you didn't last.

Tessa also developed a strong emotional attachment to Clint. Since they spent so much time together, it was only natural she would feel a growing need for him. However, lately she'd been asking him to stay—permanently.

Finally, Clint had to set Tessa straight on a few things.

"Tessa, I'll tell you this, though I thought you already understood. I'm a grown man beholden to no one but myself. I don't belong to anyone, and I'm not interested in settling down. You have to realize that I'm going to leave someday. I want to help you and I feel close to you, but I will leave."

"What about the mine?" Tessa said quietly.

Clint managed a smile. "I don't care that much about a lot of money, Tessa. You know that."

"I don't understand. You could be like Mackay or William Ralston. Start railroads, newspapers, build a business empire all your own. I... I could help you, Clint!"

He shook his head. "I'm not going to build an empire—just want to be what I am. A gunsmith. A man who can climb on a damn good horse and ride anywhere, anytime he gets a notion to see new faces and fresh country. I'm not the kind of man who wants to settle and plant roots. I sure don't want to build an empire that's going to anchor me down and make me beholden to a whole bunch of employees whose wives and children are all depending on me to make big profits. I don't want that."

"I guess I was trying to make you something you aren't," Tessa said quietly.

"I guess you were," Clint said.

"I'm sorry. I owe you everything. You're the best man I ever met, Clint. You're handsome, exciting, and brave."

"Don't stop now; you're just starting to get warmed up good!"

She laughed.

The next day, Clint finally realized that he just wasn't able to do this all himself. He decided to get in touch with Honey Bare and see if she could recommend anyone. Instead, she told him some very interesting news.

"One of the Sutro foremen came to my place of business a few nights ago," Honey began. "He got pretty drunk and he told all about how they had driven a tunnel under the Shamrock claim and were opening up a big work station. They're going to start digging tunnels up and under you. He said it would be like a catacomb."

"Who was this Sutro foreman that talked too much, Honey? Do you remember his name and which shift he works? Do you know where he lives?"

"The man's name is Bob Fortney and he works the midnight to morning shift. He's in charge of that crew. Lives at the Hotel Reno. Why all the interest?"

Clint scowled. "I'm not going to beat myself to pieces with a pick and shovel in my hands and let King Cleaver's people undermine us. Pull out all the high-grade ore that I can't reach until we get enough money to hire a full-size crew and some heavy steam equipment."

"But how can you stop a company like Sutro?"

"I don't know," Clint said tightly, "I honestly don't know."

TWENTY-THREE

Clint wanted to see this Bob Fortney and it was important that he do it before the man went out to dinner and then to work.

He hit the boardwalk of C Street and waited for Honey to catch up. "I'm sorry," he apologized. "My legs tried to keep up with my thoughts. What do you think my chances are of getting down into their mine?"

"The Sutro?" She threw back her head and laughed. "Sweetheart, nobody gets inside those big mines unless he is on the payroll and even then they watch constantly while underground. Don't think a lot of miners haven't tried to fill their pockets, their cheeks, and every other place you can imagine."

"Yeah, I was afraid of that."

"Why would you want to go down there anyway?"

He winked. "Just to raise a little hell is all."

She didn't crack a smile. "If you did manage to get into their system of stations and tunnels, you'd never come out alive."

"You could fix me a disguise."

"You're crazy!"

THE MINERS' SHOWDOWN

Clint took her arm and hurried along. She led him up to A Street and then to Fortney's hotel. Clint looked at the place and read the sign that said it was for men only. "Definitely lets you out."

"I'll wait right here," Honey Bare vowed. "If you don't come out in fifteen minutes, I'm going to get Sheriff Pierce."

He thought about that for a minute. "If there is trouble, sidestep the sheriff and find his deputy. Man named Jim..."

"Rains," she added. "It's Deputy Jim Rains. Kinda cute, isn't he?"

Clint didn't bother to answer. "I trust him alone among them," he said over his shoulder as he entered the door. "Just wish me luck."

There was no desk clerk because the hotel wasn't large enough to warrant one. There was a line of letter boxes along one wall, however, and Clint wasted no time in discovering Bob Fortney's room number. He tried the doorknob and it wasn't locked.

Fortney was a balding man in his forties, and Clint found him sitting up beside his window looking down at the red light district of town and spying on the prostitutes. There was a drink in his hands and a smile on his face. "That's old Gilroy!" he chuckled out loud and with obvious delight. "That old son of a bitch has a wife and eight kids!"

Clint cleared his throat and Bob Fortney swung around looking for all the world like a boy with his hand caught in the cookie jar. But when he saw Clint, he jumped to his feet. "Who ... why, you are ... you're the Gunsmith!"

Clint patted his holster. "Why don't you sit back down, Fortney, and have another drink. What I have to say to you is going to come a little hard."

"Get the hell out of here! If they found you in my room my life wouldn't be worth spit!"

Clint pretended real concern. "You mean King and Mace and them boys would just naturally jump to the wrong conclusion?"

"Hell, yes, they would!" Fortney started toward the door. "I said to..."

Clint drew his gun and cocked it ominously. "Doesn't matter what you say, does it? Not with me holding this gun."

Fortney gulped. He reversed direction and returned to his seat by the window. He couldn't help but look back down and shake his head, no doubt in wonder over old, no account Gilroy with a wife and eight children.

"I need a little favor," Clint said. "I want you to hire me on as your new man tonight. I want to go down to the level you're building that new station on under the Shamrock Mine."

"What ever gave you the—"

"You did," Clint said interrupting him. "You told every girl that's working for Honey Bare the other night when you had too much whiskey. Miss Bare told me."

The Sutro foreman paled noticeably. "Oh shit!" he gasped. "I can't believe I did that. They'll kill me if this gets out."

"And I'll kill you if you don't get me down in the mine."

"What are you going to do? I won't let you kill a bunch of my men. You can—"

"You let me loose and keep them away from me and nobody will get hurt."

"They will add things up and figure out it was you, the new man. And they'll learn that I let you go down there. Mace Allard will put bullets through my kneecaps and then watch me die slow. Besides, if I recognized you, someone else on my shift will, too."

"I'll be disguised. It will be dark on top and down below the light is never very good. Don't worry, I have no intention of dying down there. I'll come up with everyone else or I won't come up at all."

The Sutro foreman poured another whiskey and his bottle tinkled across the lip of his glass because his hand was shaking so badly. "Even if you weren't recognized, it would still all come crashing down on my shoulders. They'd have it figured out by noon."

"In that case, I'd suggest you take the morning stage and don't ever look back."

"I got a damn good job here! They pay me ten dollars a day! Where else in the world can I make anywhere near that kind of money?"

THE MINERS' SHOWDOWN

Clint clucked his tongue with sympathy. "Well, that is a dirty shame, but then you've been stealing from the Shamrock Mine and you have to pay the price. Besides, mining is a very dangerous occupation. Think of this as just a move to protect your health. Follow my reasoning?"

Fortney drained his glass of whiskey and grimly nodded. "Is that all, Gunsmith?"

"I think so."

"Good. Then get the hell out of my room and be at the mine at exactly midnight. I hope this disguise of yours works."

"So do I," Clint said, "or the Fourth of July fireworks are going to come a little early this year."

TWENTY-FOUR

Clint stood before the mirror and surveyed himself while the bedroom full of women shrieked with laughter and clapped their approval. They all agreed that no one could possibly recognize him and he had to admit they were probably right.

They had taken a good wig and put it on his head. The damned thing was dirty blond and he'd looked so ridiculous that even he had burst out laughing. So they'd gotten a razor and shaved the thing some until it looked like some drunken barber had strapped him into the chair and fixed him good.

The wig had made an enormous difference but then each of the girls had wanted to get her hands into making some little or not so little change. One of them had cut a thick strand of her own hair and glued it over his lip so that he had a mustache. The glue made his upper lip rise to a point in the center and he looked like a damn squirrel, but they'd all thought it was perfect and he didn't have the heart to take it off—even if he could have without ripping away flesh.

They made his eyebrows thicker and darkened them, which appeared ludicrous with the shaved wig, but they all agreed

THE MINERS' SHOWDOWN 121

that it made him absolutely a different person.

One of them got some cherry-colored gooey stuff and somehow gave him a pretty ugly looking scar across his cheek. Another begged and pleaded until he agreed to stuff his cheeks with cotton balls and that changed the entire shape of his face. One wanted to stuff more cotton up his nose to make it look wider, but he told her where she could stick the rest of the cottonballs.

Finally, they'd made him undress while each of them had raced back to her room and brought some customer's forgotten piece of clothing. He now stood in galoshes, a baggy pair of pants with white suspenders, a moth-eaten vest, and a pretty nice hat that was far too big and sat right down on his ears.

"I look like an idiot!"

Honey Bare must have sensed his humiliation and rising anger at the girls' laughter because she chased them out of her room and closed the door. He was seething.

"I meant to blend in with everyone, not look so idiotic that they all go into convulsions of laughter."

She kissed his chipmunk cheek. "No one could believe anyone would do this to himself, Clint. It's perfect and the girls had a wonderful time."

"Well, I'm glad they had great fun," he grumbled. "Do any of them know why I've subjected myself to this?"

"I told them you were going to a little costume party, that's all."

He nodded, strapped on his gun, and let Honey Bare help him into the old coat they'd selected. Like it or not, he was ready.

"What time is it?"

"It's a little after eleven."

"Then I'd better go."

"I'll go with you."

He caught her by the arm. "Uh-uh, I don't want you seen with me. If something goes wrong down there, there will be no connection as long as your girls don't talk."

"They won't. I'll make sure of that, but..."

He took her into his arms, careful not to foul up his fake mustache. "Stay here and I'll come by in the morning just to show you that I'm all right. Is King still sending you those damn flowers every day?"

She nodded.

"That, too, will come to an end one of these times. I promise you it will."

Honey Bare didn't want him to go, but she understood why he had to do what needed to be done.

Clint went out the back way and left through the alley. At the corner, a drunk miner started to approach him, probably looking to beg a little more whiskey money. Clint's face passed out of the shadow and was momentarily caught by the street lamp. The drunken miner stared at him and pulled up short. His hand fell to his side and he doubled up with laughter.

Clint snarled and hurried on past. Honey's girls had done way too good a job.

"That's far enough. You're trespassing. Back off with your hands touching the stars and keep moving."

She was in her nightshirt. There was a Winchester in her hand and Clint knew Tessa would not have hesitated to use it had he been a stranger. "It's me—Clint."

"Clint who?" She peered at him through the semidarkness.

"Clint Adams. I'm wearing a disguise, Tessa."

When she put the rifle to her shoulder and took dead aim, he spat the cottonballs out and yanked off the wig. "It is me!"

"Son of a bitch," Tessa breathed, lowering the weapon. "It is you!" She stared for a moment and then she began to laugh.

Clint tried to ignore her as he busied himself with putting the wig back on. He looked down at the dirty cottonballs and figured they weren't necessary. It took all of his will power not to rip off the itchy mustache that drew his lip into a peak.

"Are you finished?" he asked coldly.

Tessa finally got control over herself and nodded. "I'm sorry," she said, taking him by the arm and leading him into the dark tent. "But..."

After he quickly told her his plan to get down into the Sutro, she ceased to think anything was funny. "Clint, it will never work. You've never even been down in one of those places, have you?"

"No, that ought to make it interesting if nothing else."

"The Sutro is a huge maze of tunnels! You could get lost or fall down some shaft. You have no idea what is waiting for you down there!"

"They are stealing you blind, Tessa. I can't feel or see them doing it, but they are. I have this all figured out and I'm going to stop them until we hit paydirt. After that, it won't matter because you can sink your own deep shaft and King Cleaver and his crowd will have to back off."

"There's nothing I can do to stop you?"

"Do you think I'd have subjected myself to this ridiculous disguise if I were anything less than dead serious?"

Tessa placed her hands on his shoulders and looked into his eyes, then at his face. Suddenly, her mouth turned up and she couldn't help it—she was laughing again.

And that's the way Clint left her.

He stood in the semidarkness a little ways apart from the rest of a crew, which probably numbered about thirty. Several of the Sutro miners kept glancing at him but Clint ignored them. He turned his back to the huge hoisting wheel and seemed to study the massive steam engine that made his and Tessa's little fifteen horsepower engine look like a toy.

Bob Fortney was calling the roll and the miners were answering. Only a few were missing and just one man was obviously too drunk to work.

"Octojock Strongovik!"

Clint grunted loudly because it was the name they had agreed he use just before they'd parted at the hotel. The hope was that the name was bizarre enough to match his appearance and that the Poles would think he was Russian and the Russians think he was a Czech and so on so that no single nationality would try to strike up a conversation with him. Besides, the way he looked, who'd want to anyway?

"Octojock, you stick with me and I'll show you around on the fifth level. I want the rest of you to work on the third, fourth, seventh, and eighth."

"Any questions?"

"Who the hell is that guy?"

Clint turned around and smiled disarmingly. His hand slipped into his coat and through the torn pocket to rest on the butt of his gun.

Bob Fortney saw his move and swallowed noisily. "He's the new man. Now everybody stand ready to go down. We want to move forty tons on this shift and everybody is going to have to bust his butt to do it."

"Octojock, that means you, too!"

Clint grinned stupidly. He waved to the disbelieving crew and then was grateful for the huge hoisting wheel that began to spin up the cable, bringing the next crew flying up from the hot depths of Sun Mountain like a cork popping out of a bottle.

The miners were all sweating profusely and only half-clad in pants and shoes. They stepped out into the cool night air and headed for the company dressing rooms where they'd left their shirts eight hours before. Clint watched their tired, deeply lined faces in the sick yellow lamplight. They all looked exhausted. Some of them were already starting to get goosebumps and he remembered someone saying that, next to liquor and bullets, the deadliest killer on the Comstock was pneumonia. The crews came up sweating from the mine and, in wintertime, might step into a blizzard or at least a freezing wind and catch a chill.

Clint lowered his head and plowed on to the huge cage with the night crew. It was just a cage, but with a welded bar all around to hang onto. Clint noticed most of the crew were crowded into the center of the cage.

Bob Fortney pushed in last. "Better hang on tight, Octojock!"

Clint just smiled as if he didn't understand. But when the earth dropped out from under his feet and he plunged into absolute darkness he had to choke back a scream, and he clamped on with both hands.

Down, down, down they fell. For Clint, it was like a journey into hell. He couldn't help thinking he'd made a terrible mistake.

TWENTY-FIVE

Since no one else on the cage was screaming, Clint figured there was at least a small chance that the braided wire cable that lowered them was not severed and there was still hope for life. He hung on tightly and then they passed the first station. They were dropping so fast he just had a glimpse of a big open room all illuminated with lamplight; he saw two men and they yelled something that was snatched away by the roar of their descent.

"All right!" Bob Fortney yelled, his voice seeming to hang at that level.

Clint realized that Bob answered the pair, though it was a mystery how he had understood their question. They passed another station and it was the same, just a glimpse of a huge boarded cavern, men waving or yelling, and the clashing sound of heavy machinery.

The air grew appreciably warmer. And then the cage began to slow down and Clint felt as if he were suddenly becoming very, very heavy. His stomach seemed to pull down hard and he gripped the welded bar and then they were dangling in the shaft over three hundred feet below the surface.

"You men work the north wall today," Fortney ordered.

"How come? Thought we'd switched to the west wall?"

"Hell if I know," Fortney growled as six or seven men stumbled out of the cage and headed across the station. "Just do as you are told."

Now that they were stationary, Clint had a good view of a mining station and he was amazed at how comfortable a place it was. All the walls as well as the floor were boarded solid and the ceiling was heavily timbered. Along the walls were nails from which hung clothes and tools. There was a rest station with big barrels of water for the men and some crude tables and chairs for them to eat their lunches or rest at when their shift was over and they were waiting to be relieved. Clint saw big storage cabinets and they were neatly labeled with chalk. Some of them probably held blasting caps and others dynamite. One very heavy crate was labeled NITROGLYCERINE—DO NOT TOUCH!

Clint stared at that until the cage dropped again and they plunged into darkness. He had heard a great deal about nitroglycerine and all of it was bad. They said one gallon of the highly unstable liquid had the explosive power of hundreds of pounds of dynamite. The stuff was so feared that it had been outlawed in California after an accident had leveled an entire city block of San Francisco.

But it had been used successfully as well. When the Central Pacific Railroad had tried to tunnel under that highest peaks of the icy Sierra Nevada Mountains, they'd faced certain failure until they'd hired a chemist and began to use nitroglycerine. Clint had read all about it and it had seemed amazing that anything could be that powerful. And if it were powerful enough to blast a tunnel under the Sierras, it damn sure ought to be powerful enough to do anything.

They went deeper and deeper until they reached the eighth level and the last members of the crew were out and moving across this lowest station. The heat was punishing. Under his coat and vest, Clint was sweating heavily.

"How hot is it?"

THE MINERS' SHOWDOWN

Fortney said, "Almost 115 degrees. We are 1,200 feet below the surface and the plans are to go down to two thousand. At that depth, the temperatures get up around 125 degrees and the men can't work but ten or fifteen minutes at a stretch. At that rate, there's no money in it for the company."

Clint wiped the sweat off his brow. "It's a hell down here. I'm ready to leave whenever you are."

Fortney pulled a bell rope that went clear up to the hoisting operator at the surface. He yanked it five times and the cage jumped and they began to race back up the shaft.

"Doesn't your hoisting operator know any speed but this!" Clint gasped.

"Time is money. King Cleaver and his office full of accountants don't know a damned thing about this business except what they read on the ledger sheets. We have to drive these crews. They make four dollars a day, and we've tried to bust their miners union but had no luck. Thing of it is, at those wages, miners are pouring in here begging for jobs from all over the world."

Minutes later, the cage jerked to a stop at the fifth level. Both men stumbled out into the cavernous station and Fortney led the way to a tunnel that ran west. "That's it, Gunsmith. You go a hundred yards up that tunnel and you're under the Shamrock claim."

"What will I find there?"

"Why don't you follow these ore cart tracks and find out?"

Clint looked at him. "I don't believe I want to go up there alone," he said. "I had no idea of what I was getting into down here. I'm going to need your help."

"Damn it! That wasn't part of the deal!"

"I know," Clint said almost apologetically. "But I can see now that I need your help; I don't know enough to do anything but blow myself to pieces. And if I do survive, I'll get caught."

"That's your problem, not mine. You said I—"

Clint pulled his gun. "I remember what I said and I'll help you get safely off the Comstock. But you've got to help me first. I'm going to do this and neither of us wants to die down here tonight. I don't want to use too much nitroglycerine and—"

"Use the dynamite," Fortney cried. "My God, man! Only an expert touches nitroglycerine."

Clint smiled. "Well, expert, I guess we might as well get started, shouldn't we?"

Fortney stared at the gun. "Yeah," he said tiredly, "I guess we might as well do that."

"I'm glad you agree," Clint said, moving over toward one of the heavy crates with the lettered warning. "Open it up," he said.

Fortney crouched down beside the crate and eased the lid off. Inside, all packed in cotton batting, was a pair of one-gallon bottles of nitroglycerine.

"Pick one up."

The foreman gently reached inside and eased a bottle out, cupping it almost reverently in both hands. "I am scared to death of this stuff."

"So am I, but bringing that tunnel down is going to take more than dynamite."

"They'll just dig another," Fortney said in a strained voice. "Gunsmith, don't you see how big this company is? Rich people own this mine and a half dozen more almost its size. They will have that tunnel cleared and retimbered in just a matter of a few months. This isn't going to stop them. Not for long, it won't."

Clint motioned for him to stand up. "A few months will make all the difference. By then all this will be over."

Fortney looked at him strangely. "I don't know what other surprises you have in mind but I'm damn glad I'm not going to be around to see them."

"You will be if you mess this up," Clint advised him grimly. "We both will be splattered all over these rocks. Let's go."

He stood hugging the thick, yellowish fluid that rippled with a sort of oily menace in the bottle. "We'll need something to use as packing and a long—a damned long fuse. And one stick of dynamite."

"What for?"

"Trust me," Fortney growled. "I'm in this too deep now to take more chances. As it stands, we are going to need all the

THE MINERS' SHOWDOWN

luck we can get just to get out of this alive."

Clint did as he was told. He quickly found a cabinet and Fortney told him exactly what was needed. When he had everything, he said, "Sure glad I asked you to come along, Bob. I just didn't have the least idea bringing down a mine would be this tough."

His little joke, which was meant to relax the foreman so that he didn't drop his bottle of nitroglycerine, fell flat.

"Gunsmith, your ignorance about what you are forcing me to do scares the hell out of me. If you had any idea what is going to happen down here when this bottle goes off, you'd be scared, too."

"They made you the foreman over all those miners," Clint said. "That tells me you are a good man who has to know what he's doing."

"I haven't done any blasting for over three years. Even men who are doing it every day make fatal mistakes."

"I'll gamble that you'll do fine."

Fortney wasn't a bit flattered. "And even if you do get out of here—which I doubt—you'll be arrested tomorrow and sent to prison."

"Nope. You're the only one that knows it's me and not some fella named Octojock Strongovik."

"Jesus," Fortney whispered, trying to hide a thin smile as he shook his head in wonder, "I don't know where the hell you came up with that disguise and that name. Did you see the faces on my crew? They couldn't believe I'd hire something like you!"

Clint wriggled his upper lip. All the sweating he'd done since coming down here had made the glue on his fake mustache loosen. One tip of the damned thing was now hanging over his mouth. He bit it off; then spit it out. Fortney glanced sideways at him and the smile grew even wider.

I like this man, Clint thought. He doesn't know it yet, but I'm doing him a favor getting him out of a place like this. There was always room in this world for a good man to start over.

"Well," Fortney said, coming to rest in a rounded, half-timbered cavern about the size of the one that Clint worked in the Shamrock. "This is it."

He looked up. "About how far are we under the Shamrock claim?"

"I can tell you exactly. We are directly under your own shaft about 680 feet."

"Well, I'll be damned! What was the great plan?"

"Wasn't mine. I guess King and his friends figured it would be cheaper to just bore a shaft up to meet yours when you were killed or run off and Miss O'Grady sold out."

Clint frowned. "Those bastards don't miss a chance to save a dollar, do they?"

"Hell, no." Fortney walked to the working face of the tunnel and carefully placed the container of nitroglycerine down. "Now what?"

"We blow it," Clint said.

"This cavern or the tunnel?"

Clint gazed about for a minute. "I think we'll blow them both."

"Are you crazy! That would only leave the station itself. There is no telling if that would cave in or not once everything else collapses."

"I want..." Clint hesitated because he'd hoped to wait until the last moment to tell Bob Fortney what he had to say next. "Bob, I want this place, the tunnel we just walked up... and the station, too."

Fortney was staggered. "Jesus Christ, no! We won't have a snowball's chance in hell of getting out alive."

The man started backing up. He was panicked and out of control. Clint drew his gun and cocked it.

"If we've one chance in a thousand," he said, "that's one more than I'll give you right now if you take another step back and refuse to help me."

Fortney made a choking sound in his throat. He shuddered with dread and dragged his sleeve across his sweating face. But he did stop.

Clint smiled and lowered the gun. The man was no fool. One chance was better than one bullet.

TWENTY-SIX

Despite himself, Clint could not help but feel his stomach eating itself alive as they knelt beside the nitroglycerine.

They had taken turns swinging a hammer and turning a drill until they'd made a big hole that sloped down and into the wall. Now it was time to ease the jug of nitroglycerine into it and pack the stick of dynamite on top.

"At least your hands aren't shaking anymore," Clint said, passing him the gallon bottle.

Fortney took a deep breath and slid the glass container into the hole, and when that was done, he wiped his face. "Now the dynamite, packing, and the fuse."

Clint gave them to him and watched him set it up to ignite. The padding was just pressed down around the neck of the bottle and the fuse ran right on inside to the stick of dynamite.

"What about the tunnel?"

"We'll use part of the second gallon for that."

Clint dug around for a match. "Do we light it now?"

"Hell, no! We set all three charges up and cut the fuses so they go off at about the same time."

"And if they don't?"

Fortney shrugged his shoulders. "It may not even matter. The first one that goes off is going to sound and feel like two speeding twenty-car railroad trains coming together anyway. It will probably set the others off."

They placed a half-empty jug right in the middle of the tunnel and gave it a shorter fuse, and the rest they poured in an empty beer bottle and placed it at the tunnel's entrance right beside a case of dynamite.

Clint was worried. "I don't want to collapse the entire mine in," he said, "just this level."

"I know and I'm betting our own lives that won't happen. The levels are a couple hundred feet apart down here and that's a hell of a lot of rock. Besides that, the tunnels above and below us aren't going in the same direction. It'll be all right."

Clint nodded. "What about the shaft?"

"I don't know. That's the only part that has me worried. If the cage isn't on this level, I can't see how anything can go wrong. That cable wire is tough and it's unlikely any flying rock would cut or break it."

"All right, then," Clint said, rubbing his palms dry on his trousers. "What now?"

"We go back down the tunnel and light the first bottle we set up and run like hell. Then we light the one in the tunnel and run like hell again. And when we get here, we signal the hoisting operator to get us off this level before everything goes."

"What if he—ah—he's busy right then?"

Fortney shook his head. "That's where we need a little good luck. If he doesn't get us out of this station before the first explosion, we can kiss tomorrow good-bye."

"Well," Clint said, "at least no one will have to dig us a grave."

Now that it was ready to go, both men seemed calmer and more resigned to whatever lay ahead. Clint understood this very well for he had experienced this sort of icy detachment many times just before facing another fast-draw artist or famous gunman. All the talking and the thinking was finished and the

THE MINERS' SHOWDOWN

only thing left was to do what had to be done. It was that simple. You just acted.

They returned to the cavern, which Fortney had explained was hundreds of feet directly under the Shamrock. They knelt beside the fuse and Clint dug out a small box of matches. "You want the honor?"

"I've no desire to blow myself to hell. This is your idea. You do it!"

If there were a shred of doubt in Bob Fortney's mind that the Gunsmith would falter at this act, it was dispelled when he struck the match on his thumbnail and held it toward the fuse.

"That's remarkable," Fortney breathed.

"What is?"

"My hands are shaking so bad the match would have gone out and yours are steady as this mountain. I thought sure..."

"What? That I'd change my mind. Lose my nerve?" Clint just smiled. "When you have faced as many guns as I have, you learn to face death the same as life. Straight on and willing to take whatever it brings without much fuss."

Clint touched the fuse. It sputtered and just lay there almost until the match went out, and then it finally caught hold and began to spark.

"Let's run!" Fortney shouted, already twisting away and charging down the tunnel.

And run they did! Clint knew the long fuse would take a good four or five minutes to burn to the dynamite. But the tunnel was over a hundred yards long and they had two more fuses to light and then a cage to catch out of this mine.

The galoshes slowed him down and he cursed himself for not getting rid of them earlier. Now, there wasn't time. If he hadn't been a lot faster than Fortney, he'd have been left far behind.

"Hurry up!" the foreman yelled as he held the second fuse. "Damn it, run faster or I'll..."

"You'll what?" Clint asked breathlessly as he clawed for the box of matches.

"What's wrong?"

Clint swung around wildly. "They must have fallen out in the tunnel!"

"We're going to get blown up! Let's get out of here!"

Clint grabbed the man by the collar. "We've still got time. I'll go back and find the matches. You pull the rope and get that cage moving down here!"

Before Fortney could answer, Clint was running back up the tunnel as hard as he could. Fortney had said the other charges would probably go off. Probably wasn't good enough and there was a minute to spare and Clint meant to see that all the fuses were lit.

He could hear Fortney yelling at him to come back, but Clint ignored the man and kept running. He was halfway back to the cavern when he found the box of matches spilled all across the tunnel floor. Clint snatched up a handful of them and sprinted back the way he'd just came.

When he reached the second fuse, he struck a match. It didn't light. He struck a second and it snapped in two, then spluttered and died at his feet. Clint took a deep breath and forced himself to slow down. He carefully struck the third match and touched it to the fuse which ignited hungrily.

He whirled and ran again, this time clutching the precious matches in his fist.

When he burst into the station, Bob Fortney was yanking frantically on the bell and cursing. He was white as a ghost and almost crazy with fear.

"What's wrong with you up there!" he stormed. "Come on, come on!"

Clint ignored him. He thought he heard the whine of the cable unrolling, bringing the cage down to their level but he couldn't be sure. He struck a match and it did nothing. Struck three more realizing that his sweaty palms had dampened them. But he kept trying, listening to Fortney rage and listening to his own heartbeat in his ears.

Finally, a match fluttered to life and he cupped it in the palms of his hand and willed it not to die. It burned brighter and he touched it to the last fuse.

"Yes!" Fortney screamed. "Yes!"

Clint glanced over his shoulder and saw the cage dropping into view, and then he turned back and lit the final fuse.

"Oh, God, no!" Fortney screamed. "The fifth station, not the sixth!"

Clint turned just in time to see the cage flash past them on its way down. He stared at the vacant shaft and saw the Sutro foreman crumple to his knees and wail like a child.

They'd needed luck and they'd got luck, but it was all bad. Clint didn't need to be told that in his panic Fortney had pulled the bell one too many times. Sure, the mistake could be corrected. But there wasn't time for that.

They were about to be blown to smithereens.

TWENTY-SEVEN

Just as he had faced many guns in his life, so Clint had faced moments like this of sheer hopelessness. Always he'd had an instant of almost paralyzing fear and then he'd acted despite the nearly insurmountable odds against him. It was this kind of response that set the Gunsmith apart and above most other men.

Now he was running toward the shaft because he realized that it would be impossible to extinguish all three of the fuses before one of them ignited the nitroglycerine. The shaft was the only hope.

He stopped at the edge of it and peered down the long hole that dropped hundreds of feet deeper. Far, far below he could see the faint glow from the next station and the cage. It looked to be about the size of a postage stamp.

Clint grabbed Bob Fortney by the collar and dragged the man to his feet. "Come on," he shouted, "we are getting out of here!"

"How? We can't climb that cable!"

"We can at least try." Clint glanced back at the hissing fuse that was rapidly being devoured. "Are you coming or giving up?"

Just the way he posed the question seemed to give the foreman a jolt of hope. "I'm coming," he cried, leaping to his feet.

Clint stood for a moment at the precipice and balanced on the balls of his feet. He would have to leap about six feet out and then catch the cable. It was a braided wire, flat like a ribbon of steel rather than a rope. Clint had no illusions about how that cable would slice the hell out of his hands and his body right down to his legs, which he'd also be using to climb. But cuts were a whole lot better than dying.

"Here goes." He jumped and caught the rope and winced as the wires cut. He wrapped his legs around the cable and peered up the shaft. The surface was so distant, he could not see the sunlight, only the distant eye of light from the next station. He reached up and began to climb.

"Come on!" he shouted as he desperately tried to climb above the opening of the station. If he could just do that before the blast went off, then he might be all right.

He felt rather than saw Fortney's body hit the cable and then he heard a gasp of pain.

"Gunsmith, it's . . . it's slippery! I can't hold on!"

Clint knew it was the blood from his hands that was causing the problem. He was pulling himself up hand over hand as fast as he could. "Use your legs, damn it! Use your belly and every inch of yourself that you can press to this wire and quit bitching! We are almost out of time!"

His tongue-lashing goaded Fortney, and together they pulled themselves up, up until Clint was out of the lamplight and knew he was above the shaft.

"Come on, Bob! Just a few more feet and you're safe."

"I . . . I . . ."

The explosion made the earth roll and buck. One minute he was reaching up for another pull higher and the next Clint was hanging on for his very life as the entire level vanished. It seemed like one massive explosion, but it wasn't. The far cavern went first, then the tunnel, and finally the station in just the order that Fortney had planned. Clint felt himself being smashed against the boarded sides of the shaft. Somehow he hung on.

A monstrous cloud of rock and dust filled the shaft and Clint shouted in pain as splinters of rock cut at his legs, ripped through those galoshes, and ricocheted upward a few yards. But most of the solid stuff went down the shaft, not up like the cloud of smoke and dust that enveloped him in a wave. He felt himself being lifted, then whipped back and forth to crash against the sides of the shaft until he nearly lost consciousness, and the roar was like standing in a tornado.

It went on and on and when he thought he was going to faint and plummet to his death, it died very suddenly.

He pressed his cheek to the cable and choked for air that was clean. His eyes, clotted with dirt, ran with tears. Clint opened his mouth and shouted, "Bob!"

There was no answer. But then he knew there wouldn't be. The Sutro foreman hadn't been able to clear the station's ceiling in time and most likely had been bombarded with tons of flying rock.

Clint rubbed his watery eyes on the rough fabric of his sleeve. He looked down the shaft and saw nothing. He looked up and saw the same. It was dark and he hung suspended on a cutting thread over an abyss that seemed like eternity.

He had to go one way or the other, knowing full well he couldn't hang on too much longer. Clint began to lower himself because he hadn't the strength to go any higher.

If the cable was severed just below where it had been exposed to the direct force of the blast, then he was finished. But if it was not, he decided he would just keep lowering himself until he dropped on to the cage. There was nothing else he could do.

The cable was not severed. It had stopped whipping around and he swore he could feel a weight suspended from it. Clint began to lower himself even faster. He wished he could have seen what remained of the fifth station, the long tunnel, and the working face that was gutting the Shamrock, but it was dark and too dusty and there was probably nothing left to see at all.

So he kept going down and it seemed forever before he saw

a faint glow of light through the dust and realized he was finally nearing the sixth level. He heard shouts and cries of men panicked and afraid of cave-ins.

Suddenly, Clint felt the cable shudder in his bleeding hands, and then he was being lifted toward the distant surface.

For a moment he was filled with an overwhelming sense of gratitude, but then he was flooded with dread as he realized that he would be wound into the giant hoisting reel and crushed.

Clint wondered how far down it was to the screaming men hanging on the cage below. It didn't matter; he had to reach them before the cage surfaced. To fail was to die.

He forgot about the pain and began to slide. For almost a full minute he dropped; then suddenly he smashed into some kind of connector and dropped on to the mob of packed men.

They shouted and kicked at him but had no idea he'd fallen into their midst. Clint groped in the darkness and fought to stand. He was punched and he struck back like a man possessed. Someone cried out in pain, and they were flying past an upper station where a crowd of frightened miners was gathering by the shaft begging to get out.

Clint grabbed the welded rail and hung on. Those men would be all right. The nitroglycerine hadn't collapsed the entire mine, just one level as Fortney said it would.

He wished the Sutro foreman had survived to tell this story someday, even though it would never be believed.

It seemed like forever before the cage popped up and they were hit by the cold night air. Men scrambled and clawed their way off the cage, ran to the dirt, and fell to their knees to kiss it.

Clint wasn't even noticed among the miners and the crowd that was pouring down from Virginia City. Among them were two very beautiful and worried women—Honey Bare and Tessa O'Grady.

When he staggered out into the open and they saw him, they both cried with happiness and came running.

Clint kept moving his feet and met them at the boundary line of the Shamrock before he collapsed in their arms.

TWENTY-EIGHT

They both stayed with him in the tent that night and Clint was too exhausted and beaten up to remain awake any longer than it took to tell them briefly what had happened down in the Sutro Mine. In the morning he sensed the two women seemed to have struck up a friendship, maybe even a real admiration for one another.

And why not? Neither woman was the kind who'd chosen an easy road in life. Honey Bare had fallen in love only once after a tough but spectacularly successful stint as a prostitute. Her husband had run away and left her alone to fend for herself and she'd done mighty well. She was honest, caring, fair to her girls, and she was a friend to anyone who needed a helping hand.

Tessa was nearly ten years younger and more innocent. But Clint had the feeling she had the same kind of grit and fighting spirit. She could have sold the Shamrock Mine to someone and gone back to California with a trunkful of gold—but she hadn't. And it wasn't because she was greedy, either. Tessa O'Grady was stubborn; she had spunk.

THE MINERS' SHOWDOWN 141

Clint worried about both of them. King Cleaver was still sending Honey Bare daily bouquets of red roses and that meant that she was in danger. Sooner or later, the man would make a bolder move. As for Tessa, Clint figured King and his men would very quickly mount a counterattack, a reprisal for what he'd done to the Sutro.

His bizarre name and disguise might have fooled the average person, but King and Mace would know what Clint had done. They'd have no proof, but they'd know and strike back with a vengeance.

"They are going to come tonight, or the next, or the next," he told Tessa and Honey Bare, "and I'd rather you were somewhere else."

"The hell you say!" Honey Bare exclaimed. "I'm spending my nights right here by your side until this is all over."

She looked at Tessa. "That is, if it's all right with you. It is your claim."

"Are you sure you want to stay?" Tessa asked.

"Damn sure." Honey Bare looked at the pair of Winchesters that had never been reclaimed by the two Sutro guards. "I know how to use those."

"So do I," Tessa said grimly. "Let them come!"

Clint scowled. He should have guessed they'd react like this. "If I can't change your minds, maybe someone else can. I don't want either of you down here at night."

"This is still my claim," Tessa argued. "You can't kick me or my friend off."

He studied his bandaged hands. "No, I don't suppose I can. All right, since I can't hold a pick or shovel for a while, you'll both have to do the mining and heavy work. But first, you can start right here."

"What do you mean, right here?"

"Just what I said. If there is an attack, it will come at night and be fast and heavy. There are too many people around here for them to stay more than a minute or two. My guess is that they'll riddle the tent with bullets. Our best chance at survival is to be below the ground level where their shots can't touch us."

Honey Bare looked down at the floor of the tent. Tessa had

spread out some sacking and a few rugs, but it was easy to see that the ground was more gravel than dirt and the digging would be tough work. "How far below ground level are you talking about?" she asked skeptically.

"Oh, we need an area big enough for all three of us to sleep in. Should be three feet at least."

"Be like a damned grave," she said.

But Tessa just laughed. "No, it won't! It will be real cozy, the three of us in there."

Clint was watching Honey Bare closely. The woman was used to silk sheets and breakfast in bed. The hardest work she'd probably done in years was to change the linen. "You sure you want to stay down here?"

Honey Bare wasn't sure at all, but she did have a whole lot of stubborn pride. "Course, I am! I said I was, didn't I?"

"Yes, but . . ."

"But nothing, Clint. Where is the damned shovel?"

Clint grinned. Watching these two luscious women pound rock and haul it away was going to be entertaining. It was funny how life always threw a man the damnedest little diversions.

The attack came two nights later and though Clint had thought they were ready for it, they weren't prepared for the sudden and awesome firepower that unleashed itself on them. One minute they were lying there asleep and the next they were listening to rifle bullets tearing across every square foot of their tent, ripping it to pieces and blowing holes in their provisions and their cooking utensils and making their water barrel leak like a sieve.

Clint was in the middle, which suited him just fine. Earlier, he'd been able to fool around with them both without either being aware that the other was having a good time. But now, as the barrage of lead slashed their tent and everything above ground to ribbons, he held them both close and waited.

Suddenly, the firepower died.

"Roll up and get ready!" he gritted, reaching out of their pit and grabbing his pistol. With the bandages on his hands, he couldn't hold it very well yet, but could still point and fire.

THE MINERS' SHOWDOWN

If Mace and his men had any notion to finish them off, they were going to be in for one hell of a sudden surprise.

They waited but all they heard were shouts from the hillside and thundering hooves.

Tessa was up first and crawling toward the ragged tent entrance. "They're leaving!" She gaped at the destruction. "They figure that not even a skinny old rattler could have survived in here."

All three of them felt somehow victorious—that is until they saw what the raiders had also done to their machinery.

Tessa was furious. "Damn it! They know we can't work this claim without that hoisting equipment and now look at it!"

Clint held the lantern up. "The boiler is riddled, and some of the other parts are busted and shot up, but we ought to be able to repair them."

"We are running out of time and money, Clint. That note is due in less than a month."

"I'll lend you the money," Honey Bare said.

"No," Tessa said quickly.

Clint looked at her. "Pride is a good thing to have, but not when it stands in the way of good sense."

Tessa's chin quivered. It was easy to see the struggle that was going on inside of her. She finally looked Honey Bare in the eye and said, "I'm owner of this claim and I'll sell you half for enough money to pay off the note due to King Cleaver and to replace this boiler."

"I don't need..." Honey Bare began.

"That's the only way I'll do it," Tessa blurted.

"You heard Clint say that Sutro was working ore right below us. We are sitting on a fortune here."

"And if we ever reach it, well, I think there is room for another millionaire owner."

Clint said, "Make it a partnership. That's only fair. I supply the muscle, Tessa the brains, and you, Honey Bare, you supply the money we need to beat King Cleaver. What do you say?"

"I say it's a deal!"

"Good." Tessa seemed especially relieved. "I think we should have papers drawn up for the partnership so that it's legal and binding."

Honey Bare protested but Tessa seemed determined, so a decision was made to have papers drawn and the deed re-recorded in all their names.

There was one other decision that was made and it came from Honey Bare. "I don't know anything but what I hear every night in my place listening to my clients, but it seems to me we need a bigger steam engine. And some help."

"No one will sign on to help us," Clint said. "I've already asked around town. Even offered to pay higher wages. The word is out and we are outcasts on this hillside."

Honey Bare frowned. "What about the machinery?"

"You are talking about a lot of money."

"I have a lot of money, Clint."

"To do it right is going to take about twenty thousand in cash."

Honey Bare swallowed. "That is a lot of money. But I can do it."

"Are you sure?"

She nodded. "I just might have to go back to work myself on a very selective basis."

Clint thought she was kidding. But when he looked at her face, he wasn't so certain.

TWENTY-NINE

Two mornings later Honey Bare dressed in her finest and left her establishment. Like most successful boom-town madames, she dressed flashy, preferring lots of red and black lacy materials, gold jewelry, and ostrich feathers. Unlike most madames, she was still relatively young and quite beautiful. She was also very popular among the men of the town for her generosity and public good works.

"Afternoon, Miss Bare!" repeated itself over and over as she headed down the boardwalk, swinging her hips and holding her silk parasol.

She liked men and that was the difference between most women in her business and herself. Honey Bare didn't often come across men whom she did not care for, but today she was going to meet two of them and the first was her banker, Mr. Bainsworthy. She would have dropped the man years ago, but he'd lent her the money for her start here on the Comstock and she had remained a customer of the Bank of Virginia City out of stubborn loyalty ever since.

When she entered the bank, she asked for its president and

was shown into the man's office at once. She made him nervous. He kept looking through the glass of his office and worrying that one of the respectable, wealthy wives of a Virginia City mine owner would see this popular madame with him.

Honey Bare knew this and it made her dislike the hypocrite even more. "If you prefer, you could come to my place of business after hours,"

He blanched. "Uh...no, thank you, Miss...Miss Bare. What can I do for you?"

No formalities. No small talk even though she had been one of this man's best customers over the years. Honey Bare decided she really had to leave this bank and find another, but first, she needed a loan.

"I'd like to borrow some money," she told him. "About ten thousand dollars ought to be enough in addition to my entire savings which I will withdraw right now."

His brittle smile fractured. "Miss Bare! That is a lot of money!"

"I know that."

"But—but why?"

"Personal reasons. Of an investment nature."

His ears perked up. Honey Bare knew this man was a heavy investor in mining stocks that fluctuated wildly and could make or break someone within hours.

"Have you—ah—" He cocked his head. "Have you heard of something you might like to share?"

She smiled. The old bastard was really interested, sure that she had gotten some fantastically hot tip from one of her more prominent clients. Honey Bare saw her opportunity and grabbed it.

"I might," she winked knowingly, "if and when I get the loan."

He sat up and did a fine job of hiding his disappointment. "You shall have it at once! Your credit and rep—your credit is impeccable. Excellent payment record."

"My girls are the finest."

His mouth dropped open and his face went beet red. Honey Bare had to bite her lip sharply to keep from laughing at the expression on his face.

THE MINERS' SHOWDOWN

From that moment on, he could not seem to get rid of her fast enough. She took her money in cash and rose to leave.

"Wait!" He mopped his face nervously. "About that . . . tip."

"Tip? Oh, yes. You may tell your boss, who I am sure is Mr. King Cleaver, that I am using this money to pay off the note he holds on the Shamrock Mine." Bainsworthy rocked back in his swivel chair and stared at her. She continued, "I suppose that one of these days, now that I have an equal partnership, the mine will issue stock. Ought to be wildly profitable, wouldn't you say?"

He didn't say anything. He just sat there as if he'd swallowed a bone and it had lodged in his windpipe. If Honey Bare had had any earlier doubts about his connection with the Sutro Mining Corporation, they were gone now.

She took over thirty thousand dollars cash and marched out the door with a triumphant smile on her face. However, it was a smile that quickly faded because she was determined to face King Cleaver and at last have a long overdue showdown. She would pay off the note he carried on the Shamrock Mine and tell him to stop sending her red roses every morning.

When Honey Bare reached the offices of the Sutro Mining Corporation, she halted and took a deep breath. She'd have given anything if Clint were here with her now and...

"You sure took your time," the familiar voice said.

"Clint!" Honey Bare almost threw herself into his arms. "How did you know that I was—"

"A fortune teller," he explained jokingly. He then added, "Truth is, I know you too well."

"But you can't go in there with me! You did once and it was a miracle that you came out alive. I won't let you do this."

"I brought some help." Clint pointed across the street, and out of a general store came the sheriff's deputy who was carrying a couple of parcels. Tessa stood at his side. "I thought we might as well make a party out of this."

Honey Bare laughed and felt as if a great load had been raised from her shoulders. With the deputy and Tessa along, even King Cleaver would be powerless to have them shot or taken prisoner.

"Why not," she said, waving to Tessa happily. "When we

pay off that note, we all ought to be there to see their expressions."

They marched into the Sutro headquarters and a hush fell. Clint saw a young man leap out of his seat and head for a door labeled CONFERENCE ROOM but he stepped in front of him.

"We need no announcement," he said, shoving the door open.

They were all in there. King Cleaver at the head of a long table and his men sitting down either side of it. And the nearest to him was Mace Allard.

Clint remembered Tessa's description of what one man had done to her the night he was gone, and it took all of his willpower not to draw and shoot Mace where he stood. He didn't draw, fearing the man might outdraw him right now with his bandaged hands and that a stray bullet would strike Tessa or Honey Bare.

"Mace, don't even think about it," the deputy warned. "Not unless you want to hang."

The hired gunman's hand edged away. "The time is coming," he hissed. "I haven't forgotten what you did to me. And we know about your trip down—"

"Shut up, Mace!" King Cleaver was on his feet. His little, deep-set eyes were on Honey Bare and he licked his lips and spoke to her as if she were alone. "So, we finally meet again. You are more lovely than I remembered, Miss Bare. Do you like the flowers?"

"No, but my girls do."

King's smile dissolved. He looked genuinely injured. "But I thought... the man who delivers them said..."

"That I was pleased?" Honey Bare laughed coldly. "We stick them in our chamber pots."

King's complexion turned slate. He began to shake with an almost uncontrollable fury that was not helped when Honey Bare threw an envelope filled with money in his direction. It hit the table and slid its length.

"It's for the note you hold on the Shamrock Mine. We'd like it back now."

King gripped the table with his fat, little fingers until they were bloodless. The demons inside him raged to be free. But

THE MINERS' SHOWDOWN

he beat them down and choked, "Get the note, Arthur!"

A small, bookish man jumped out of his conference chair and vanished only to reappear a moment later with the note in his fist.

"Give it to them, Arthur!"

Honey Bare took it and gave it to Tessa. Then, to everyone's shock and amazement, she marched around to stand before Cleaver. She was less than half his size, but there was a controlled fury in her that made her seem much larger. "You sick son of a bitch," she whispered, "no woman in her right mind would let a monster like you touch her. You make my flesh crawl and you always have." She turned away then and left him spitting and gasping like a man gone berserk.

Clint followed her out and then the deputy. Everyone was in shock but Tessa. She stood at the door and said, "You're an evil man, King, but I do feel sorry for you."

Their eyes met for a long moment and then she walked out of the room.

The very next morning, something happened that Clint would never forget. The young deputy came riding down to the Shamrock Mine and dismounted. He looked drawn and haggard and seemed to have aged considerably since the day before.

The moment he saw him, Clint felt a cold chill pass through his body and he was filled with dread. "What's wrong?"

"It's Honey Bare." He looked away.

"Is she..." He cleared his throat. "Is she dead?"

"No, but she has every right to be. Someone came into her room last night and beat her over the head. She didn't see who it was. They stole a great deal of her money and set her bedroom on fire. By all rights, she should have been burned to death."

"It was King Cleaver's people," Clint gritted. "You know it and so do I."

"Of course, it was. Just as everyone knows you were the man who blew up the fifth level of the Sutro Mine. But I'll tell you what I told King that next morning—we need proof."

"Maybe you do, but I don't," Clint said. "I'm going up to see Honey Bare. Then I plan to pay another visit to the Sutro headquarters."

"That's what they are counting on," the deputy said. "You won't get ten feet in that door before you'll be Swiss cheese."

Clint pushed by the man. "I can't let them get away with this!"

"Hold it!"

Clint spun around. "Don't try to stop me," he warned.

The deputy thought it over, then shrugged.

"All right," he said finally. "I can't be the next sheriff of this place if I'm buried in the cemetery. But before you go off half-cocked, I have something to show you."

Tessa came to join them. "I overheard," she whispered. "I'm sorry, Clint."

"These belong to you," the deputy said, after untying a box from behind his saddlehorn. "Western Union saw me coming down and I told them I'd deliver."

Tessa opened the card that was attached to the box and read it aloud. "My dear, lovely Miss Tessa O'Grady—I had never realized how very beautiful and kind you are. I will give anything to possess you, to make you my Queen. Anything!" The note was signed, your favorite King.

The note fell from her hand and Tessa stared down at the box. No one had to tell her what was inside. The deputy grimly opened it. There were three dozen red roses.

Tessa looked away. When Clint touched her shoulder, he could feel her trembling.

"Well, Gunsmith, are you ready to start using your head again?"

He nodded. It was a miracle that Honey Bare was still alive. Now, it was Tessa's turn. She needed Clint more than ever.

THIRTY

"I'm flat busted," Honey Bare told him from her bed. "But I'll come back."

Clint looked down at her. She looked just fine except for a huge, turbanlike bandage wrapped around her head. "I wish I could just go over there and clean that nest of vipers out."

"The time will come. And when it does, I think that young deputy, Jim Rains, will help you and maybe even the sheriff as well."

"Sheriff Pierce is in King Cleaver's back pocket, just like half the other officials in Virginia City. Rains might help, but none of the others will."

He looked down at the woman. "Are you going to be all right?"

"Sure. I've hired some bodyguards. As you might imagine, I have no trouble getting men to work for me. The fringe benefits are rather exceptional and the pay ain't bad either."

Clint had to smile at that. He had seen two tough men posted outside the door in the hallway. He just hoped they paid more attention to their duty than to the half-clad girls who were always lounging around.

"Don't worry," Honey Bare said, "I'll make sure that they do their job. Besides, you can see the big, sliding bolt lock I had put on the inside of my door."

He looked at it. It was obviously the best money could buy. "Looks like it would stand up to a battering ram."

"Latch it, Clint."

"What..." Clint smiled. "Honey Bare, you are not a well woman."

She had thrown back the covers and she was wearing only a smile.

"Make me well again, Clint."

The way she put it, he did not see how any man could say no. Clint was out of his own clothes in a minute and latching that new door lock so that they wouldn't be disturbed while he made her feel better. It had been too long since he'd had time to pleasure this woman, and she'd earned all he could give her.

Honey Bare held her arms out for him. She admired his body, and after lying beside him down in that pit on the Shamrock Mine, she was eager.

He sat on the bed and bent forward and kissed her, pushing his tongue into her mouth. A moment later, he moved down until his lips were brushing her nipples, first one and then the other.

Honey Bare drew in a deep breath and closed her eyes. She was already hot and her hips were starting to rotate in an easy circle. When he began to nip at her nipples, she gasped and pulled his face into her ample breast. She let him have all he wanted of them and it was she who finally could stand it no longer and reached down to grab his cock. She was breathing fast.

He shifted position. Then she felt him opening her legs and his warm, probing tongue was licking her in a way that made her heels drum the sheets. Honey Bare pulled his legs onto either side of her face and looked up at his throbbing manhood. She licked her lips and raised her head and it was like eating fruit off the tree. When she took him in her mouth, she felt his whole body shudder. She began to suck, using the length of his shaft in a way that was extraordinarily pleasurable.

The harder she sucked the more frantic his own tongue

worked at her, and Honey Bare began to feel the exquisite pleasure building in them both.

He was doing to her even better than she was doing to him, so it became an unspoken challenge to her to make him climax first.

She tore her mouth away and began to lick him like candy, and when his hips began to churn as fast as her own, she laughed. "I'll beat you this time, Clint!"

He pulled his head up and said, "You are ready now! Honey, you haven't got a chance."

Before she could answer, she realized that she was going to lose again to this man. She felt her belly begin to twitch, her hips were bucking, a hot fire was exploding inside, and she was crying out in pleasure, urging him not to stop. For several moments, she could do nothing but lie there.

"You won, damn it," she finally panted. "You always win."

She didn't care, not really, and to prove it, she reached up and took almost all of him in her mouth and worked him up and down until his hips were soon jerking out of control and he was roaring with pleasure.

When he rolled off her and turned back around, they both smiled with satisfaction.

Honey Bare said, "I always was about fifteen seconds faster. Someday, I'm going to make you come first."

He kissed her breasts. "That's a day I greatly look forward to, my dear. And the kind of race no man would mind losing."

"I suppose not." Her smile faded. "Clint, I imagine you heard that I was robbed of every penny I had."

"I didn't know the amount. That bad, huh?"

"I'm afraid so. Old Bainsworthy must have told King that I'd withdrawn all my savings. It was foolish but I was going to hand it over to you and Tessa today. Kind of make a little party over our new partnership. I had visions of spreading that twenty-two thousand dollars across the bed and then all three of us having a wonderful time making love on a blanket of greenbacks."

"You have some strange fantasies, Honey Bare. I don't think Tessa would have gone for it."

"You never know until you try. But it doesn't matter now.

The Shamrock money for repairs and improvements is all gone. I've barely enough to repair the fire damage and keep my girls fed."

"We'll get by somehow. You paid off the note, at least. And as for the bullet-riddled machinery, well, we will find the money someplace."

"Maybe you can win it at cards again."

Clint shook his head. "That kind of thing only works once. There's not a gambler on the Comstock who'd get suckered into that kind of game with me again."

She looked at his hands. "They're about healed."

"Yeah, and it's a good thing, too. I need to get back down in that mine and get to work."

"But how can you without a steam engine?"

"We'll use Duke and a set of winches to raise and lower a bucket of some kind. If I can just strike a little bit of paydirt, then we can quickly earn enough to fix the boiler."

Honey Bare nodded. "Doctor says I have to stay in bed, Clint. Sure wish you did, too."

He kissed her mouth. "I'll be up to visit whenever I've got the strength. And as soon as I hit some paying ore, you'll be one of the second to know. I'll buy you some flowers and—"

She shook her head vigorously. "I've seen enough flowers—especially red roses—to last a lifetime. Bring Tessa and champagne when you strike paydirt, Clint. And we'll all celebrate."

Clint decided not to tell her about the roses that Tessa had just received from King. It would only upset Honey Bare to learn that poor Tessa had replaced her as the object of King's desire. So he decided to laugh and make a joke. "As long as you are not thinking of the three of us celebrating in this bed. One of you at a time is enough for any man."

She reached down and tugged playfully at him. "For any ordinary man, Clint. But not for you."

Clint could not help swelling a little bit with pride.

THIRTY-ONE

He worked three more weeks and they didn't make a cent. Clint pounded at the west end of the Shamrock Mine until his hands were tough as boot leather and his muscles were hard. He had never been an especially muscular man, but he had a smooth catlike agility and strength that was deceptive. While other men might have bigger arms and shoulders, none could react as fast as he could and his endurance had always been exceptional—in bed or out of it.

But one evening as he sat beside the campfire, he felt as if perhaps they were whipped. "We haven't enough money to buy food, Tessa."

"We've still plenty of flour, sugar, coffee, and beans. We can make it another week or two. I know we can."

Clint nodded wearily. He wasn't going to quit until they had to, and Tessa was working almost as hard as he was. "I just feel we are doing something wrong," he said.

"Maybe we ought to try another tunnel off in the other direction. Might change our luck."

They both heard someone coming across their claim. "Get down in the hole, Tessa!"

Clint grabbed his gun and moved away from the campfire. "That's close enough. Stop right there and announce yourself."

"Myself is Scotty Herman and I am in the company of the sweetest girl you ever laid eyes on."

"What's her name?"

"Daisy."

Clint holstered his gun and stepped back into the firelight. "Come on in and join us, Scotty. Coffee is on the fire."

"Hell with coffee. Whiskey is what puts a man to sleep at night. Whiskey and women."

Tessa laughed. "We've got one of them." She walked out to greet the old prospector, threw her arms around his neck, and gave him a good squeeze. "I'm glad to see you!"

His eyes shone. "Glad to see you, too, Tessa. You sure are a good-lookin' woman. Your father would be proud of you. Proud of the way that you growed and how you came back. But he would call you a fool for not selling this old hunk of rocky ground. You ought to sell out, Tessa, sell out before something bad happens."

All the gaiety went out of Tessa and she went to find a bottle after the old prospector had conned her out of a cup of sugar for his burro.

Scotty cupped the bottle and drank before lowering it and coughing. "Good stuff!"

"Keep it," Clint said. "There is plenty more where it came from."

Scotty studied him closely. "You hit any good dirt yet?"

"Nothing."

Scotty nodded and glanced at Tessa. "Why don't you sell out? I know someone who'd give you a fair price for this claim."

"Who?"

"Secret. But his money is good. You could make enough to consider yourself rich. That's more than I ever got from it."

"It's not for sale," Tessa said. "Not now, not ever. We were just talking about trying to tunnel in another direction. West isn't doing a thing for us."

Scotty took another drink. He frowned with obvious concentration as he swallowed the whiskey down. "Think you ought to keep diggin' west."

Clint was surprised for some reason. He'd have thought the old prospector would have told him to try another direction. "Why?"

Scotty studied his gnarled, work-busted old hands. "Why not? Most people say the main drift of the ore is to the west under Sun Mountain."

"But it isn't even—"

Scotty jumped up and exploded in anger. "First you ask me for my advice, then when I give it to you, you wanna argue with me! I'm getting the hell out of here. Sorry I came. Come on, Daisy. Let's leave these damn fools alone in their misery. Don't know good advice when they hear it."

Tessa ran up to him. "Scotty, please, don't rush off. I'm sorry you're so upset. But we are, too. If we don't start hitting some paydirt pretty soon, we're finished."

He relaxed and nodded. "Sell the claim, darlin'. Sell it while you can and get off the Comstock before it's too late."

They watched him disappear into the night, and he was working hard on the whiskey.

"He's going downhill fast," Tessa said miserably. "I hardly recognized him. He used to be a hell of a man."

Clint just shrugged. "Sure did seem determined that we ought to sell out."

"Well, we aren't!"

"Which direction do you think we ought to work?"

Tessa frowned. "We won't leave, but I will take his mining advice. If it's all right with you and Honey Bare, I think we ought to keep tunneling west."

"Fine with me," Clint said. "Down there, all directions look the same and one seems as good as the other."

At about the same time the very next evening, Scotty showed up again. He looked awful and Clint guessed he had probably gotten even more whiskey someplace. He was still sober enough to talk, however.

"I need a job."

"Here?" Clint frowned. "Hell, man, haven't you heard about what King Cleaver would do to anyone who helped us?"

"Piss on Cleaver!"

Tessa poured him some hot coffee. As he cupped it to his mouth, his hands were shaking badly. "We can't even pay you, Scotty. Not right now we can't."

"Pay me in whiskey, keep Daisy in good hay, and that's enough."

"I think we can handle that," Clint said before Tessa could answer. "I need some help, need someone to show me how to use dynamite."

Scotty cocked one eyebrow and squinted knowingly. "Whatsa matter, bub, ain't got no nitroglycerin' layin' 'round down there?"

"Afraid not."

"Got dynamite?"

"Some."

"Good. Work will go even faster. Steam engine don't work?"

"Boiler needs fixing," Clint said.

"Too damn bad. Without an engine, no use in using the dynamite. Couldn't get the ore out the hole anyway."

He staggered over to the winches and sized up the method they were using with Duke. "Hell of a waste of good horseflesh," he grunted. "They use this kind of setup down in Mexico. Poor man's steam engine. It's nothin' but horseshit."

"It's the best we've got," Clint said irritably. "You want to work with me or not?"

Scotty stared at him with red, bleary eyes. "You shoulda sold out like I told you—gotten clear away from here and taken the girl to someplace safe."

Clint had heard enough. He was stiff and sore and tired, and he didn't need to listen to this kind of talk. "I'm going to bed, Tessa. Give him some whiskey and maybe he'll go away again. He's good at running."

At the crack of dawn he and Tessa awoke to the smell of a fire and fresh coffee brewing. Scotty was mixing some flapjack batter and humming some song Clint had never heard before.

He looked bad, but good, too, in a comforting sort of way. Clint sure hadn't expected him to stay.

"Get up, you two lovebirds!" the prospector rasped. "Breakfast is about ready and the Shamrock ain't going to work its damnself!"

Tessa groaned but they both got up and dressed quickly in the tent. When they stumbled outside, the sun was just peeking over the horizon.

Clint raised his arms and stretched. "You going to help me do some work today, old man?"

"I'm going to work your young ass off," Scotty growled. "I'm going to show you how a real miner moves some ore."

Clint and Tessa exchanged glances. They had a feeling they were in for one hell of a rough day.

THIRTY-TWO

Two weeks and more than a hundred tons later, they still had not hit paydirt. Clint had never worked so hard in his life. He was astounded at the stamina of the old prospector and wondered how much work he'd been able to do in his younger days.

It was back-breaking labor. Scotty would hold the steel drill and Clint would swing his nine-pound hammer. He was always afraid he'd miss, hit the old miner's hand, and shatter his bones, but somehow, he never did. One thing was sure—as long as Scotty was drinking whiskey at night, he wasn't about to trade places with the old goat. One miss and Clint would never again use his hand to do anything more than stir water.

Clint and Tessa were sitting by the campfire one evening, wondering how many more days they could hold out, when Scotty came rushing back from town all excited.

"Did you hear the news?"

Since Scotty wasn't a man given to showing much interest in anything, both Clint and Tessa sat up and took notice.

"What news?"

"There's gonna be a big drillin' contest this next Sunday up on C Street! Winners get two thousand dollars. Second place team gets a thousand."

Clint leaned forward with interest. "How does it work?"

"Real simple. They give everybody a chunk of the hardest old granite they can find, then they fire a gun, and everybody starts hammering and turning the steel bit so it don't bind in the rock. An hour later, they fire the gun again. Them that haven't given up and are still swinging their hammers have their holes measured. Deepest hole wins the two thousand."

Tessa's voice betrayed her excitement. "Clint, I know you have lots of stamina," she said with a sly wink. The way she said it made his cheeks warm, but it was too dark for anybody to see his embarrassment.

Scotty was confident. "What do you say, partner? We ready to win two thousand dollars in prize money? That's enough to buy a hell of a lot of whiskey, hay, and beans."

"I don't know," Clint hedged. "Half the miners on the Comstock will be competing for the prize. Men a whole lot more experienced than I am."

"Sure, but about half of 'em will be drunk and won't last the hour. A whole bunch more will be too afraid to swing hard for fear of hitting their partner's hand and smashing it. A miner can't work with a busted fist. He'll starve on the Comstock or be forced to leave."

Clint was still dubious. "In the first place, I don't even know if I can last a full hour."

"You can if you pace yourself and I'll count slow enough for you to finish without even breaking into a lather. You can do it."

"I'll be struggling at the end. When your arms start to cramping, you get wild. I could miss, Scotty. I could hurt you bad."

"I'll take the chance, gawddammit! I need the money and so do you."

Clint had run out of arguments. He didn't want to think about how punishing such a contest would be, yet the worst that could happen would be that he'd collapse in exhaustion and not be able to finish. But if he could win... even win second place money, it might be just enough to carry them on to paydirt.

"All right," he said finally, "I'll do it!"

"Woooweeee!" Scotty yelled, "now you're talking. We got three days to practice up."

"What do I need practice for? Swinging a hammer is all I've been doing for the last month or two."

"Sure, but now I'm going to teach you the finer points. You may be the Gunsmith everywhere else, but come Sunday, you're going to be the world champion hammer swinger."

The way he said it, Clint was almost ready to believe him.

Sunday came around too fast for Clint. He stopped working at noon on Saturday and trudged up the hill to visit Honey Bare. She was sitting up in her bed reading a column on the tricks miners use to cheat their bosses.

"This fella is a genius," Honey Bare said with a wide grin and tears of laughter filling her eyes.

Clint looked out the window. They were bringing the blocks of granite in on big wagons and parking them the length of the street. Clint could not help but feel a twinge of nervousness. The contest was all the town was talking about this week and it was his secret goal just to finish. Most people agreed that if fifty men started, no more than seven or eight would last the hour.

"Clint, honey, don't you worry so much about tomorrow. You and old Scotty will do just fine."

"You ever see one of these drilling contests?"

"A couple."

"Pretty rough?"

"No," she laughed. "Most of the contestants are too drunk to do much of anything. They just get up there in the wagon and make a spectacle of themselves for everybody. It's a lot of fun to watch. There will only be a few teams that are serious about the contest. Usually one from each of the big mines."

Clint frowned. The big mines employed hundreds of drillers. His chances didn't seem that good. Still, if he was getting up there at all, he was going to go all out to win. That was the only way he knew.

THE MINERS' SHOWDOWN

"Go lock the door," Honey said patting the bed next to her.

"Uh-uh," he said, "not today. If I win, then we can get together tomorrow."

Honey Bare looked disappointed. "If you win," she said knowingly, "you won't have the strength to climb the stairs to my bedroom, let alone do anything to me."

Clint nodded. She was probably right.

He chose a wagon right under Honey Bare's window because she could have her bed shoved over to the window and cheer him and Scotty on to victory.

It was a warm day but there was a good, strong breeze and that was going to save the contestants for at least a while.

The crowd numbered in the thousands. They'd come from Reno, Carson City, the sawmills all along the Carson River clear up into the Sierra foothills. Yelling and hooting, they were having a high old celebration. Standing up in the ore wagon with Scotty, Clint wished he were a spectator and not a participant.

All the wagons were filled with teams and the contest was about to begin. A trio of judges had come around and inspected the drills and the hammers, though Clint could not imagine how any team could possibly cheat. Other than drilling the hole, the only way to get through that rock was to use dynamite and no one was going to get away with that.

"All right," Scotty said, taking their first drill in both of his hands and setting it down on their block of granite, "you just start slow and work to my beat. An hour of swinging steel is going to go by mighty, mighty fast if you don't burn yourself out in the first few minutes the way some of these fellas will do."

"Why is it I don't believe you?" Clint asked with a smile.

He looked at Tessa. No one else was allowed in the wagon except the driller and his holder and they could not exchange positions.

"You're going to win!" Tessa called. "I know you will."

Clint nodded. The crowd grew silent and all eyes turned to the contest chairman who raised a pistol to the sky and cried, "Ready."

Clint took a deep breath. He looked up at Honey Bare who shouted, "Get 'em, honey!"

"Set."

Clint raised his hammer like the other contestants.

"Go!" And the pistol unleashed a puff of white smoke in the air as the crowd cheered eagerly.

Clint wanted to rush. He began to swing too fast and realized that so many people were shouting that he could barely hear old Scotty calling a slow beat up to him.

"One. One. One. Slow—down!"

Clint forced himself to slow down, even though his heart was beating like hell and urging him on. He concentrated on Scotty's call and his hammer fell into a steady, rhythmic beat that did not vary at all. Down below, people were shouting at him to go faster.

He could hear other hammers ringing against steel and he was going much slower than they were. He picked up the beat just a hair.

"No! Damn you, Clint. Listen to my beat!"

Clint gritted his teeth. It was all he could do not to throw down his hammer and tell this old coot to go to hell. He didn't like being yelled at and he was damned sorry he'd ever let himself get talked into this mess in the first place.

Sweat began to bead on his forehead and roll down into his eyes and it stung, but he ignored it. Tessa's voice became just one in the crowd, and even Honey Bare, who was screaming herself hoarse, seemed to fade into the background.

He only heard old Scotty's count, and after a while, even that seemed to fade as he locked into a rhythm that had no beginning and no end.

Clint thought of Lake Tahoe. He could picture its deep blue water and see the rocks and the fish—see the reflections of clouds floating across the surface like big sailing ships. The pines were whispering a lullaby to him and he felt the cool mountain breeze on his skin. It felt wonderful.

"Pick it up!" Scotty was yelling as he twisted the steel bit around and around keeping it from binding. He was also pouring water into the deepening hole and that kept the drill from getting too hot and snapping as well as dulling any faster than

THE MINERS' SHOWDOWN

necessary. They were allowed four drills and no more. Scotty could replace them so deftly that Clint was amazed to see that he was already through the first two and working on the third.

"Pick it up!" Scotty was yelling. "Damn it, man, we are in this thing! Listen to me now and pick up the pace!"

Clint began to swing a little faster as Scotty hurried the beat a fraction. He was bathed in sweat and his ears were ringing like the steel, but otherwise he felt damned good. I am going to finish, he thought with pride.

"Time?" Clint shouted, "how much time is left?"

"Fourteen minutes," Tessa cried, "just fourteen minutes! Clint, you're both doing wonderful. There are only six other teams still in the contest."

He smiled with grim satisfaction as his confidence soared. He was going to finish—maybe even win! Scotty had been right. The key to this was pacing oneself.

Clint picked up the beat again. The crowd sensed it instantly and cut loose with a roar of approval. It made Clint's blood race faster.

But suddenly, a high piercing scream cut through his senses, overrode the crowd's yelling, and made him glance up toward Honey Bare who was leaning out of her bedroom window and pointing directly across the street toward a window. Clint's hammer missed and smashed into the granite, but Scotty's hands weren't there to receive the blow.

The old prospector was throwing himself at Clint—hitting him in the chest and knocking him, sprawling, into the wagon as two rifle shots boomed overhead.

Clint wasn't wearing his gun. It was down in the wagonbed and out of the way so he could compete. But now, as Scotty's body jerked under the impact of the bullets meant for him, Clint was diving for his holster, rolling in the wagonbed, and coming up to fire.

The ambusher was swinging his weapon to bear on Clint, trying to fire at this elusive target. He was too late. Clint triggered off five bullets and each of them tore into the man's chest. He staggered against the window. Thousands saw him drop the rifle and his hands flutter at his vest as if trying to plug up the bullet holes.

He was still trying when he pitched forward, somersaulted, smashed through an awning, and crashed into the street.

Clint twisted around to see Scotty. The man was dying.

THIRTY-THREE

Clint had seen enough gunshot wounds to know that old Scotty Herman was going fast. The man was shot right through the lungs, and as the crowd was shouting for a doctor, Clint saw Scotty feebly motioning him to bend down and listen to his dying words.

"Swear to me you'll take care of my Daisy," Scotty gasped, taking hold of Clint's arm and squeezing it powerfully.

"I swear it," he promised.

Scotty blinked. He looked up at Tessa, now also beside him in the wagonbed. "Don't cry, girl. I ain't worth your tears."

"Yes, you are."

Scotty wearily shook his head. "You don't know I was your Judas!"

"What do you mean?" Clint leaned closer.

Scotty turned to stare at him. His eyes were beginning to glaze. "Mace Allard made me keep you working on the west wall. They're hoping you'll go broke and have to quit. They made me try to get you both to sell out."

"But why'd you do it, Scotty?"

"Gonna kill Tessa and Daisy if I didn't. Poison her. Shoot her with a rifle. He coulda done it easy. Nothing even you could do to stop him, Gunsmith. Nothin'."

Clint nodded. Scotty was right. During all the hours he spent down in the shaft Tessa was unprotected.

"Gunsmith!"

"I can hear you, old-timer."

"Start..." he coughed and bloody bubbles formed on his lips. "Start working the north face of the Shamrock! North face!"

"I will."

"And... and get to hammerin' steel. Gotta win the two thousand dollars for us so... so we can be... champions!"

Clint watched the prospector. He was staring up at the blue Nevada sky, but he was sightless. Still, maybe he could hear that old familiar ring of hammer on drill and it would send him away in peace.

"Grab the drill and hang on," Clint gritted.

Tessa understood perfectly. She placed their last sharp drill down in the hold, and as the Gunsmith raised his hammer the crowd cheered. His hammer rang loud and strong and then Tessa was calling out the beat faster and faster.

And that's the way they finished. Clint was driving steel and Tessa turning it round and round and the dust was flying out of that granite block in neat little puffs.

"It's over, Clint! It's over!"

She jumped up and threw her arms around him, and he let the hammer fall into the street below where men fought over it as a prized souvenir.

"Clint, you and Scotty won!" Tessa was sobbing.

It didn't matter to him right then—not when he looked down at Scotty and saw him smiling in death. They'd finished. That's what really counted.

But fifteen minutes later, the judges made it official. They had won!

Clint looked up at Honey Bare and saw the sun glistening on her cheeks and knew she was crying. He took the money from the contest judges and picked Deputy Rains out of the crowd. "Help Tessa get this safely to any bank on the Comstock except the Bank of Virginia City," he ordered.

The deputy nodded, helped Tessa down, and then led her away.

Clint stood up in the wagon and the crowd kept cheering his victory. But it brought him little pleasure because Scotty was dead. They had never been close; maybe now he understood why the old prospector had always been so tormented and unfriendly. He'd been haunted by his own guilt, the guilt of a Judas.

Clint's eyes lifted over the crowd, and he saw the man who had made Scotty's life a hell these past few weeks.

Mace Allard was staring up at him, and when their eyes locked, Clint just nodded and began to strap on his holster.

Mace Allard had lived way too long.

Clint reloaded his gun and the crowd fell silent. They followed Clint's stare and saw Mace Allard standing down near the Delta Saloon, and when Clint spun the cylinder on his gun and let it drop lightly into his holster, they knew.

He jumped down and the crowd parted, leaving an open corridor straight to Mace Allard who was moving off the boardwalk and out into the dusty street.

Clint's hands were swollen and thick from the hammering. He worked his fingers, trying to beat some life back into them. His arm muscles were all tied up and they felt as if they weighed a hundred pounds each. He wasn't ready to face a professional gunfighter. Wasn't ready at all. His blood-swollen right hand wasn't responding and his fingers were numb from an hour of gripping a hammer and then taking the shock of thousands of blows. The palms of his hands were still covered with the scabs from the Sutro mine cable.

He's going to beat me, Clint thought. He's as fast a man as I've ever gone against and I could beat him if I was ready, but I'm not and he's going to kill me right here in the street—the best that I can do is to stand up and take him along with me.

"So," Mace said with a grin as he came to a halt on C Street. "I guess some kind of congratulations are in order."

Clint stopped. "Scotty told me what you had him do."

"Get it in writing? Huh? Too bad, Gunsmith. How do your

hands feel after that? A little stiff and numb? That's a damn dirty shame."

"I'm ready whenever you are." Clint didn't want to hear any talking. He blocked out everything except the man who stood poised before him—the man who was finally going to outdraw the Gunsmith.

Mace Allard's hand suddenly streaked for his gun. Clint moved on reflex alone, but his cramped arm could not respond fast enough and even as his own numb fingers slapped the butt of his gun, he knew he was just not going to make it this time— knew that he was beaten, not by much though. Mace wouldn't have stood a prayer under normal conditions, but..."

A shot boomed over the crowd and Mace, gun halfway out of his holster, was lifted up and thrown over backward. He skidded in the dirt, then rolled around, and still tried to fire, but another rifleshot kicked him back in the street. This time he was finished.

Clint stood there for a moment. Then he pivoted on his heel and gazed across the street. His eyes lifted to meet Honey Bare's. She was holding a smoking Winchester.

THIRTY-FOUR

Sheriff Pierce arrested Honey Bare and she was jailed for murder. However, when the local newspaper interviewed her and reported why she'd killed Mace Allard, the public outcry in her favor was so overwhelming that no one on the Comstock doubted that she'd be freed, perhaps even given a commendation.

Clint visited her every day. Her girls had been allowed to come to visit, and they'd fixed her jail cell up as nice as they could. It looked just like a rich woman's boudoir. Pink curtains hid the window bars; there were flowers everywhere and good paintings on the walls. They'd even hidden the unsightly cell bars from view by hanging lush, red velvet drapes.

"The only thing I haven't got here is you, Clint, darlin'," Honey Bare complained sadly. "I've talked myself blue in the face and that damned old sheriff won't let you come in and spend the night. I need some lovin', honey!"

Clint shrugged. "We wouldn't have much luck trying to do anything between these bars. Guess you and I will have to sit tight and wait it out. Your trial is just a formality. You'll be free as soon as it's over."

She came over to grip the bars and be near to him. "I know, but... but I've been here a week now and all I can think of is you and me together again. What do you say we lock ourselves up somewhere for a while once I get out? Just the two of us with no distractions."

"How would you like to go back to Lake Tahoe and help me finish my vacation? Got to buy a new tent, but otherwise we are all set."

Honey Bare kissed him quickly through the bars. "It's a deal!" She pulled back. "How is our mine coming?"

"Very well. After you killed Mace, three good men came over and said they wanted to work for us. King Cleaver must be going crazy."

"Does he still send Tessa flowers?"

"He won't stop."

Honey Bare shook her head with worry. "Much as I hate to say this, stay real close to her, Clint. Don't leave her unprotected."

"You think King will try something?"

"I do. The moment he thinks the game is up, he'll act. And when he does... when he does there is no telling what will happen. The pig is insane."

"I know. With Mace Allard gone, I sometimes get to thinking that we won—but we didn't. The man has at least three or four others like him on the payroll. A day of reckoning is just around the corner. I can feel it."

"You be careful, too."

"I will. I'm almost glad you are in jail. You're in the safest place you can be until this is all over. Deputy Rains will keep the sheriff and the others honest."

She nodded. "If anything happened to me in here, the miners would lynch Sheriff Pierce and he knows it. Don't worry a thing about me. Just be careful and find some gold!"

"I'll do my level best," he promised, "I surely will."

Just three days later while working the north wall of their new tunnel, Clint's pick broke through a sheet of rock to uncover a wall of quartz, mica, and gold. For a moment, he just stared at it in disbelief and then he let out a whoop of celebration while the other three miners he'd hired beamed.

He stepped back and grinned broadly. "One of you cut me out a hunk of that ore so I can take it up and surprise Tessa."

And that's what he did. Rode the cage up and there she was working the hoisting wheel as always. Clint jumped out of the cage and walked right over to her.

"Congratulations, Tessa!" he laughed, "you and Honey Bare have struck it rich!"

Tessa just stared at that big chunk of gold-riddled ore and then she began to cry.

As was the custom whenever any new strike was made, Clint and Tessa had to go up to C Street and buy drinks on the house for the Comstock miners. But first they stopped by the jail to tell Honey Bare the wonderful news.

"Son of a bitch!" she whispered with reverence. "I knew it. I knew it! I told Taffy; I said, 'they're going to strike it rich and have the biggest celebration you ever seen and I'm gonna be locked in this damned old jail.' Son of a bitch!"

"Just think of it this way," Tessa said, "at least you'll stay out of trouble and get a full night's sleep. Probably feel a whole lot better than Clint or me in the morning."

But Honey Bare just shook her head in sorrow. "Biggest damn party in my life and I have to miss out on it. Not everyday a woman like me becomes rich."

"You were already pretty rich before you got robbed," Clint reminded her, hoping to lift her spirits.

She did manage a smile. "That was different. Took years of saving. This is practically overnight. That makes it a lot more exciting. Besides, it's more fun being rich with a partner. Hell, we could all three have gone up to my room later and . . ."

"Honey Bare . . ." Clint growled a warning.

"Could have done what?" Tessa asked.

Honey Bare looked down. "Had some imported champagne I keep for special occasions."

"That would have been fun. I'm sorry about this. But the champagne will keep, won't it?"

"Sure," Honey Bare said, trying hard to brighten, "and I'll even send one of my girls to chill it so that it will be perfect."

"Good," Tessa said, obviously relieved that her partner seemed to be perking up. "Well, Clint, the town is waiting."

"I'll be out to join you in a minute."

"Look," Clint said when they were alone with those damned bars between them, "I feel lousy about this."

"Ah, you and Tessa run along and have a great time. I'll be out of here in just a few days and the champagne will just taste that much better."

Clint wasn't buying it. "I've an idea," he said. "I'll talk to Deputy Rains. If he is on duty later tonight, I'll see if he won't let me bring some of that champagne in for a visit."

Honey Bare's smile was radiant. "You mean we could—"

"If you can get a couple of your girls in here to cover this wall completely so the deputy doesn't learn any new tricks, that's exactly what I mean."

She took a deep breath and laughed. "Never did it in jail before! And don't worry about the champagne; it will be here on ice, and that will be the only thing around here that won't be hot!"

Clint nodded. Subtle, Honey Bare was not.

It was close to midnight when Clint was finally able to get away and climb back up the hill toward the jail. The night was clear and the air warm but with just the taste of fall. Clint was thinking about how he and Honey Bare might have to buy some warmer blankets because nights would be getting pretty frosty up in the Sierras. He thought they might be able to count on perhaps a month more of good weather and then they'd have to come back down.

After that, he thought he'd find a good home for Daisy and then travel on. He was getting a little restless again. As for the Shamrock Mine, well there were plenty of good men that Tessa and Honey Bare could hire to ramrod things—men who knew a whole hell of a lot more about mining than he ever cared to learn.

When he got to the jail, Deputy Rains was ready and waiting. He grinned and shook his head. "Man, I won't even think about what that woman is going to do to you in there! She's got a six-course dinner waiting and champagne up the gazoo.

THE MINERS' SHOWDOWN

But if you ask me, you're gonna be her main course!"

"Well, I didn't ask you," Clint replied. "Now, why don't you go keep watch over Tessa. When I left, she was sleeping. Had a little too much to drink during all the celebrations up and down the street. Just keep an eye on her."

"Gladly!"

Clint caught him by the arm. "Don't wake her up, Jim. And don't get any romantic ideas."

"Oh, you can't keep a man from having ideas. But don't worry. I'll stay away and be a gentleman, if that's what you're worrying about. I just don't know how you can handle them both at the same time."

"I can't," Clint said with a wink of the eye. "Now get out of here and don't come back until first light."

As the deputy turned to leave, Clint jammed a solid gold nugget the size of a rifle bullet into his pocket. Having the chance to cheer up Honey Bare tonight was worth that and more.

They ate quickly behind the red velvet curtains and neither of them really tasted the food nor the rare French champagne. Honey Bare was in the pink negligee that she loved to show herself off in, and Clint thought, despite the setting, she had never looked more desirable.

Her hair was all piled up on her head and he took her into his arms and loosened it to cascade down around her shoulders. Then he untied the string around her neck and let the silken garment slip from her perfect shoulders and fall to her ankles.

Honey Bare was so eager she was trembling as she fumbled with the buttons to his shirt, then impatiently began to tear them away. Clint let her.

She fumbled with his belt, then undid his pants and pushed him down on the bed, and knelt to pull off his boots.

"Oh, Clint, you don't know how much I've been wanting this."

"I've been looking forward to it, too," he said. "Nothing on earth could keep me from being here alone with you tonight. Nothing."

Honey Bare gazed up at him with desire burning in her eyes.

Then, she lowered her head and—

"Gunsmith! She's gone! Tessa is gone!"

Clint jumped up and grabbed his pants and boots.

Honey Bare yelled, "Oh, Clint, why now!"

"Because he waited until I was gone, that's why! King Cleaver must have had someone watching me every minute."

He yanked on his boots and strapped his gun around his waist. "If I can, I'll be back tonight."

"Just save her from that madman!" There was a current of hysteria in Honey Bare's voice that made Clint leap out of the cell and charge for the door. He remembered every grotesque detail of Cleaver, his piggy little eyes and womanish mouth and his sick fondness for Chinese boys.

But now he was consumed by desire for Tessa O'Grady. And when she fought him, screamed and called him names, and humiliated him as Honey Bare had done—when she did that—there was no telling exactly what would happen.

THIRTY-FIVE

Clint raced out of the sheriff's office after slamming Honey Bare's cell door behind him.

"Clint!"

He didn't have time to argue with the woman. There was enough to worry about tonight without Honey Bare's coming to help and getting herself shot in the bargain. Clint had grabbed a rifle from the gun cabinet, knowing there was a chance that he'd be using it on the sheriff himself before the night was over. Pierce was working for Cleaver, and tonight he'd have every man on his payroll armed and waiting.

Clint took the first horse he came to and swung into its saddle.

"Hey! You're stealing a horse!" Jim Rains said.

"Borrowing it! Come on, this is no time to quibble!" The deputy wasn't very happy about this but he could also see the logic. He was sweet on Tessa and he knew where she'd be and what would be her fate in King Cleaver's mansion.

Together, they galloped down C Street and headed straight for that ugly mansion on the hill. Big jagged spears of lightning split the sky and stabbed into the barren hilltops. There was a storm coming over the Sierras, and his shirt flapped open because it had no more buttons thanks to Honey Bare's passion.

But the Gunsmith cared nothing about those things and his entire concentration was focused on the challenge that lay just ahead. King Cleaver would know he was coming, maybe alone or maybe with friends but coming nonetheless. Reaching Tessa wasn't going to be easy.

They came up to a mine and Clint sawed on the reins.

"What are we stopping for?" Deputy Rains shouted.

"Dynamite. Make the night watchman get us a half dozen sticks. We'll never reach Tessa without it!"

"Now, wait a minute!"

Clint drew his gun and started toward the supply shack. It was locked as he knew it would be. He pointed his gun at the lock and the deputy shouted, "No!"

"Then get the damned watchman to open it. Quick!"

In moments, they were back and the door was opened. Clint rushed inside and came back with an armful of dynamite. "You got any matches?"

Deputy Rains swallowed. "Yeah."

Clint shoved three sticks under his belt and remounted his horse. He gave the deputy a couple and spurred off again, not interested in a debate.

They tied their horses at the same gully where he'd left Duke once before. "We better split up and come at them from opposite directions. If one of us goes down, the other has to reach the upstairs and get Tessa out of there. I'll take the front because that's where most of them will be waiting."

"Good luck," the deputy said. "If we do pull this off—"

"Not 'if' but when," Clint corrected. "That girl's life is in our hands. We can't afford to fail."

And that's the way they parted. Clint levered a bullet into the breech and he was ready for however many men stood waiting just ahead. He looked up at the second-story bedroom windows and whispered, "I'm coming, Tessa. Just hang on."

Tessa awoke, her head pounding fiercely and a ball of terror rising in her throat. Someone had slipped into her tent and struck her with an object that had knocked her unconscious. She wished she did not have to come awake. Before she even opened her eyes, she had the sick realization that she was tied and naked on King Cleaver's bed.

She was afraid to look—afraid and quite certain that if she opened her eyes, she would find herself staring up at him and that he would just be waiting to use her.

She could almost smell him over the sickly sweet scent of burning incense. And then she felt his hand touch a breast and she shrank with a gasp.

"So, my dear, you are awake!" He leaned very close, close enough that she could taste his breath on her face. "Open your beautiful eyes."

She squeezed them tightly. His fingers began to curl into the soft mound of her flesh. The pain built and built until she moaned and her eyes flew open.

His fingers relaxed, then began to stroke her. "You must learn to obey me," he said with sweet tolerance. "I never will hurt you, my love, but I cannot stand disobedience."

Tessa swallowed. The man was insane. She could see a wild craziness in his eyes and he kept licking his lips and playing with a breast. His fingernails were long and almost pointed and they hurt.

He was wearing a black, Oriental smoking jacket made of silk and decorated with dragons. His own sagging breasts were almost as large as hers because he was so fat.

"Please," she begged pulling at the cord that held her bound and vulnerable to whatever he wanted to do to her, "untie me and let me go."

"Oh, no," he said with a frown, "you must be taught at once how to pleasure me."

Sheer panic welled up inside her and it was all she could do to keep from screaming over and over again. She desperately wanted to spit in his bloated, repulsive face and shout curses at him, tell him what a sick monster he was and how her flesh was crawling at his touch.

"I can do wonderful things to you, Tessa. Wonderful things I have learned from the Orientals that no western brute like Clint Adams would ever guess were possible. And I'm going to show them to you right now."

"No, please," she whispered. "Let me go. I won't say anything about this to anyone. I promise."

"I don't believe you. Not yet." His fingers with those long, manicured nails shifted to her other breast and began to play with it.

"You see, my love, I have decided to marry you tomorrow."

"No!"

"Yes. And when we are married, the Shamrock Mine will finally belong to me."

"I have a partner."

"Not after tonight. The whore—well, I have made arrangements." His eyes burned with hatred.

"What are you going to do?"

"Have her killed, of course."

"Please, I'll—I'll do whatever you say if you'll let her live. I'll do anything!"

His fingers abandoned her breast and she felt them glide down across her belly and lower. She was trembling so badly he must have noticed how horrid she found his touch.

"Anything?" His fingers began to play with her; he twisted them around and around. She wanted to go crazy!

"Yes," she choked, "but please don't kill her—or Clint!"

"Show me right now what you can do, Tessa. Show me right now."

He stood up and slowly pulled at the sash and his black robe. When the knot was undone, he pulled the robe open and revealed his stiff manhood.

Tessa closed her eyes. She was going to be sick if she had to look, and if she vomited, he would kill them all for certain.

"My darling, open—"

A tremendous explosion rocked the mansion, shook it as if it had taken the force of a war cannon. Tessa heard him squeal with rage and then he was leaping toward the window. A second blast seemed to knock out the legs of the mansion and she felt the entire structure lurch and sway.

He staggered across the room and grabbed a small pearl-handled pistol from a bureau drawer. He was cursing terribly as he hurried back to her.

THE MINERS' SHOWDOWN

"Please," Tessa begged, struggling at her bonds. "I'm what he wants! Let me go and he'll leave you alone!"

For a moment, as he stood there, a mountain of hideous fat, layer upon layer, she thought he was going to shoot her. But then, to her horror, he sat down beside her and placed the gun into her quivering bellybutton. The steel was cold as ice and she clenched the silk sheet.

He smiled very sadly. "Yes, my dear, it is possible we both may have only a few moments more to enjoy together. So... so enjoy them we must."

She couldn't help it any longer. She began to scream hysterically.

THIRTY-SIX

Clint threw the last of his sticks of dynamite at the scattering men, and when it exploded, it took the entire porch and just blew it away like a pile of matchsticks in the wind.

He dropped to one knee and worked the rifle until he could see nothing moving except a few survivors who were escaping.

Two more explosions suddenly rocked the night and he knew that Jim was still alive and coming. Clint threw down the rifle and drew his gun, then sprinted toward what was left of the porch. It was on fire now, flames licking the edges of the walls. Time was going to run out fast.

He shot through the front door, which hung feebly on its hinges. The entry was torn to pieces, furniture blasted to bits, pictures destroyed, even the wallpaper was hanging in ragged shreds.

At the top of the stairway, two of King's best gunmen suddenly appeared and opened fire. Clint threw himself to the side and his gun belched fire and smoke. Both men collapsed and smashed over the railing to the floor below. Neither one of them was the sheriff.

Clint could hear Tessa's screams and he jumped for the

staircase and took it three steps at a bound. He struck King's bedroom door with his shoulder and his momentum carried him and the door into the room.

Clint hit the floor rolling. He saw King next to Tessa, twisting his great blubbery body around in panic. His gun looked almost like a toy in his fist. Clint shot the man and his first bullet plowed up and under his breast and only seemed to make him shudder. The gun in his hand fell forgotten as he tried desperately to get out.

Clint's mouth twisted and his gun thundered again and again until that ugly monster was rolling over backward and crashing off the great bed. When he struck the floor, it shuddered.

Tessa was sobbing uncontrollably and Clint threw a blanket over her, then quickly untied the cords. Smoke was coiling up the staircase. It was the only way down short of jumping from the second-story window, and Tessa was in no condition to do that.

He picked her up in his arms and staggered toward the doorway. They poised for just a moment at the head of the stairway. Flames were roaring in the parlor and they would have to break through a wall of flame to reach the outside. Clint prayed that the deputy had cleared out the opposition because if Cleaver still had any hired guns out there waiting, he and Tessa were as good as dead.

It was like hurling through the gates of hell. For one terrible moment, he felt as if he were on fire, but then he was crashing into the dirt and rolling as the flames rushed past and up to the second floor.

Clint pushed himself onto his elbows and clawed for his gun. He didn't need it. Deputy Rains was there and he was alone, beating the flames off Tessa's blanket and rolling her over and over in the dirt until she was all right.

"Clint, Honey Bare is in trouble! She's going to be murdered!" Tessa choked.

He staggered to his feet—made himself twist around and start running for their horses. He should have guessed—should have known!

Locked in that jail cell, Honey Bare was safe from all but one man—Sheriff Pierce!

Pierce had her bound and gagged and was loading Honey Bare in a wagon in the back alley when Clint stepped into view and softly called his name.

The man looked up, his face reflecting his shock and wild terror. Then, because he knew it was over, that he would either hang or go to prison, he made his play.

The Gunsmith was expecting the move. He went for his own weapon. It came up fast and a bullet caught Sheriff Pierce in the shoulder and spun him completely around. When the old lawman tried to lift his pistol for another shot, Clint shot it out of his hand and left him kneeling in the dirt, moaning in pain over his shoulder wound and his ruined hand.

Clint untied Honey Bare and pulled the gag out of her mouth.

She threw her arms around his neck and kissed him as if he were life itself. She looked up at his singed and smoke-blackened face and shook her head.

"You look terrible—and yet wonderful. Does that make any sense at all?"

"I guess so."

"I heard the explosions. When the sheriff came rushing in, I knew that you were winning. Did you . . . ?"

"Yeah," he said wearily, "King Cleaver is dead and Tessa is going to be all right in a few days."

"Look!" Honey Bare pointed to the north. There was a straight line of alley running clear to the edge of town, and they could just see the massive fire on the hilltop. In less than an hour, it would be nothing but ashes if the storm didn't bring a quick and drenching rain.

Clint moved over, grabbed the sheriff by the coat, and hauled him to his feet. He dragged him back around and into the office, then started to push him into Honey Bare's open cell.

"Not this one," she said. "Put him in one of those over there."

Clint threw the man into a stark cell and locked the door. When he turned around, Honey Bare was back in her own lush cell. She was holding up the red drape in one hand and beckoning him with the other.

"Champagne is cold and I'm still red hot," she said in a

voice throaty with desire. "We never quite got around to that celebration."

The bone-weariness fell away from Clint just as Honey Bare's negligee did. He smiled and guessed he'd earned a celebration.

After all, he thought, stepping into her cell as the drape fell to give them total privacy, it wasn't every day a man saved the lives of two beautiful, sensuous women friends.

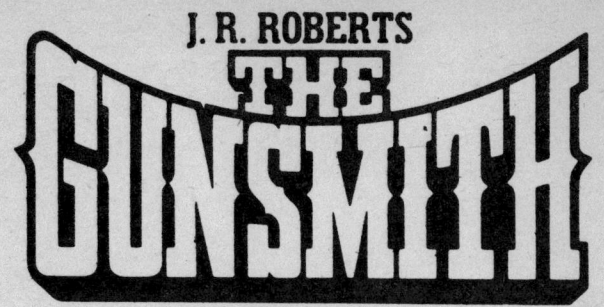

J. R. ROBERTS
THE GUNSMITH
SERIES

☐ 30896-1	THE GUNSMITH #25: NORTH OF THE BORDER	$2.50
☐ 30897-X	THE GUNSMITH #26: EAGLE'S GAP	$2.50
☐ 30900-3	THE GUNSMITH #28: THE PANHANDLE SEARCH	$2.50
☐ 30902-X	THE GUNSMITH #29: WILDCAT ROUND-UP	$2.50
☐ 30903-8	THE GUNSMITH #30: THE PONDEROSA WAR	$2.50
☐ 30904-6	THE GUNSMITH #31: TROUBLE RIDES A FAST HORSE	$2.50
☐ 30911-9	THE GUNSMITH #32: DYNAMITE JUSTICE	$2.50
☐ 30912-7	THE GUNSMITH #33: THE POSSE	$2.50
☐ 30913-5	THE GUNSMITH #34: NIGHT OF THE GILA	$2.50
☐ 30914-3	THE GUNSMITH #35: THE BOUNTY WOMEN	$2.50
☐ 30915-1	THE GUNSMITH #36: BLACK PEARL SALOON	$2.50
☐ 30935-6	THE GUNSMITH #37: GUNDOWN IN PARADISE	$2.50
☐ 30936-4	THE GUNSMITH #38: KING OF THE BORDER	$2.50
☐ 30940-2	THE GUNSMITH #39: THE EL PASO SALT WAR	$2.50
☐ 30941-0	THE GUNSMITH #40: THE TEN PINES KILLER	$2.50
☐ 30942-9	THE GUNSMITH #41: HELL WITH A PISTOL	$2.50
☐ 30946-1	THE GUNSMITH #42: THE WYOMING CATTLE KILL	$2.50
☐ 30947-X	THE GUNSMITH #43: THE GOLDEN HORSEMAN	$2.50
☐ 30948-8	THE GUNSMITH #44: THE SCARLET GUN	$2.50
☐ 30949-6	THE GUNSMITH #45: NAVAHO DEVIL	$2.50
☐ 30950-X	THE GUNSMITH #46: WILD BILL'S GHOST	$2.50
☐ 30951-8	THE GUNSMITH #47: THE MINERS' SHOWDOWN	$2.50

Prices may be slightly higher in Canada.

Available at your local bookstore or return this form to:

CHARTER BOOKS
Book Mailing Service
P.O. Box 690, Rockville Centre, NY 11571

Please send me the titles checked above. I enclose _____. Include 75¢ for postage and handling if one book is ordered; 25¢ per book for two or more not to exceed $1.75. California, Illinois, New York and Tennessee residents please add sales tax.

NAME _____

ADDRESS _____

CITY _____ STATE/ZIP _____

(allow six weeks for delivery.)

A1/a